WINDS OF THE CUMBERLAND

BODIE & BROCK THOENE

Publishers Since 1798

THOMAS NELSON PUBLISHERS
Nashville

Published in Nashville, Tennessee, by Thomas Nelson, Inc

ISBN 0-7852-8075-8

Printed in the United States of America

1 2 3 4 5 6 7 QPK 05 04 03 02 01 00 99

*To the memory of Jesse Dodson,
whose true story this is, and to
Jesse Wattenbarger
Jess Thoene
Jessica Rachel Thoene-McCraw
and
Jessie McCraw*

CHAPTER 1

$\mathcal{N}$ASHVILLE
FEBRUARY 1862

It became clear to me as I crossed over the Cumberland Mountains that the Confederate forces beyond the stronghold of my home territory of East Tennessee were in trouble.

Three days into my journey to Nashville I heard the tales of Southern defeat from a wagon train of a dozen refugee families fleeing the inevitable.

I introduced myself. "Jesse Dodson, McMinn County. What news from Nashville?"

"Nashville is doomed to be abandoned by the Confederacy!"

"They say a hundred thousand Yankees are closing in!"

"Nashville is no place to go right now, Dodson! There's a Yankee sharpshooter behind every tree!"

I thanked them for the information and the warning, then pressed on into the gathering gloom of twilight. I was dressed in civilian clothes and had little fear of Yankee snipers. Anyway, my boy was gone, the Union was advancing on Nashville, and I intended to fetch William back home!

As I rode on the rain pierced me with a chill as sharp as a sniper's bullet. On the west side of the Cumberland Mountains I stopped at a coaching inn to rest and feed my horse, Trafalger.

The inn was no more than a large log barn with a fireplace at one end, a few plank tables where meals were eaten, and a separate room where boarders were given cornhusk-filled mattresses to lay on the bare dirt floor. All the same, it was shelter from the bitter cold winds that swept down from the slopes of the mountains. A night beneath the stars could be pure misery.

That evening a dozen soldiers in Confederate gray ate their meals in silence, scraping spoons against tin plates with such ferocity that I wondered how long it had been since they had eaten. These were no holiday soldiers. Their clothing was stained from hard travel. Gold braids were tarnished, and scarlet trim was faded from heat and cold and hard service in the field.

They paid me no mind as they tore off chunks of coarse brown bread and sopped up the last drops of gravy from the venison stew. The proprietor was a grizzled old woman. She carried the kettle of vittles around once again and told each man to eat up for they would need their strength to fight the cussed Yankees.

When she looked my way at last, I smiled in a friendly fashion and held out my bedroll to show my intentions.

She cocked an eye at me as if she did not approve of my civilian clothing. "Where you headed?" she asked.

"West. To Nashville."

The sergeant was a young man with chapped, wind-burned skin and fair hair and eyes. I figured he could not be much older than nineteen, and yet he had the weary and drawn expression of one who had seen far more suffering than any man should see in a long lifetime. He raised his head and sized me up. "Going to fight the Yankees are you?"

I replied truthfully, "The Yankees have my boy, and I will fight to get him back if I must. He is a child of sixteen."

"A prisoner," the sergeant said through a mouthful of bread. "Blue bellies are taking our boys captive every day. Taking them north across the line. You don't have much chance of finding one among them all."

"I promised his mother I would try."

The sergeant nodded. "You'll have a deuce of a time getting through our lines and over to the Union side."

"I'm a civilian."

"It's plain to tell you're a Tennessean."

"McMinn County."

"We'll hold your part of the state all right. But Nashville?"

"It is not going well for the Cause then?" I asked.

He motioned for me to come sit beside him and his companions and he would give me all the news.

I paid the proprietor two and a half dollars in Union gold for my lodgings and a meal of stew. Taking a seat close to the fire, introductions were made, and the grim story of Union aggression against Tennessee was recounted.

"We hear Brigadier General don Carlos Buell, in command of the Federal Army of the Ohio at Louisville, has been ordered to march against Nashville with fifty thousand men. Fort Donelson on the Cumberland River is under heavy attack. We twelve are all friends and neighbors from Alabama and have been on furlough. News of this situation reached us, and we have been riding for three days to rejoin our unit in Nashville. These are perilous times. There is safety in numbers. You may ride with us tonight if you wish, sir."

I thanked the sergeant and explained that Trafalger was in need of rest and that I must stay until morning. Left unsaid was the fact that my son William was one of the blue-coated Federal troops.

It came to me that this serious but kindly natured fellow and his comrades might be the very men who would raise their rifles and fire upon my son. This caused me tremendous grief at the foolishness and waste of this war. Shaking the hand of each soldier as they departed, I wished them well for the sake of their families. They were fine young men, not much older than my son.

I spent a restless night with thunder rolling above me like artillery fire. Finally, I rose before dawn to resume my journey through the downpour.

From the start of the rebellion, William had been determined to join Lincoln's army against the wishes of his mother and me. "This is not our war one way or the other," I told William after Fort Sumter was shelled. "We own no slaves and owe no loyalty to either batch of fools! The son of Jesse and Alcie Dodson will not raise a hand against friends and neighbors in McMinn County, Tennessee. 'Thou shalt not kill,' the Good Book says, and you'll join the Yankees over my dead body!"

Next morning, in spite of my threats, William was gone. He left his mother a note:

> Dearest Mother,
> Father cannot understand, but I aim to fight to see Nashville beneath the banner of freedom for all in our country or die trying. I will not war with Father just to fight for the Union, so I am leaving quietly. You know in your heart it is right that I do this. Forgive me, dear mother. Pray for us and for freedom. Farewell until we meet again . . . perhaps on Jordan's further shore.
>
> Your son, William Dodson

William had never even seen Nashville nor traveled fifty miles from our farm. I blamed his foolishness on an English Methodist Abolitionist Sunday School teacher who preached Abe Lincoln. This London reformer had filled William's head with nonsense and then left with a vow to return someday wearing a Yankee uniform to set every slave free. Now, so had William.

As for me, I had not voted for the Giant Killer, Lincoln, for President. But neither had I voted for the fire-eater, Breckinridge, nor for Stephen Douglas, the Little Giant. Instead I had taken my place with most of my state and county and voted for Bell, a well-spoken, moderate Tennessee politician of the Peace Party. (I shook his hand once at a Knoxville rally.) How I regretted that Bell did not win. Things might have been different.

Whatever the cause, William had broken the heart of my wife, Alcie, when he left. I promised her whatever the odds I would try to find him. This matter alone meant far more to me than the coming Northern invasion of my home state.

The muddy road was rutted from last night's passage of wagons and cannon and the tramping of army boots, but by midmorning the highway was nearly deserted. A dozen overloaded civilian buckboards passed me heading the opposite direction. From the passengers I learned that the Yankees had completely encircled Fort Donelson and it was only a matter of time before "The Bonnie Blue Flag" would be heard no more in Nashville.

Travel-weary and hungry, I arrived in Nashville early on the morning of February 15. It was bone cold, gray, and drizzling. I led Trafalger to the livery stable where an agitated young stableboy, a slave of about sixteen years, took the reins then stood peering out the barn doors toward the direction of the market square.

Over the rooftops the mournful cadence of a bell tolled the call for assembly.

"I ain't never heared that bell make such a queer noise before," muttered the colored boy in a fearful tone.

"A church bell," I remarked impatiently. "It's the Sabbath."

"Nawsir. It ain't Sunday. It's Saturday t'day." He shook his head. "That there's the market house bell. Don't ring 'less somethin' be burnin' down. Ain't no fire though."

"Where's the boss?" I asked.

"He done gone to the square. They's all gone. Reckon they intends to fight the Yankees. Bossman say our soldiers all a'runnin' south away from them Yankees."

The voice of the stableboy was tinged with such sorrow over the imminent fall of Nashville that I was certain it had not occurred to him that the coming of the Yankees would mean his freedom.

I instructed him to stir himself and tend to my mount. "Yankees or no Yankees, that critter is hungry and so am I. Where's a good inn?"

He directed me to the Brown Hotel, where I hoped to find a hot breakfast and lodgings. A mob of ashen-faced citizens scurried past me to the square, where some momentous news about the war was to be announced. The streets were full of activity. The lobby of the hotel, however, was completely deserted. Dining room empty. I noted full plates of breakfast left uneaten and abandoned.

I considered the wasted food for a moment then scooped up eggs and ham between two biscuits and downed a cup of still-steaming coffee.

After satisfying my hunger, I joined the throng on the boardwalk. Making my way up the street, the tolling bell brought to mind the grim clang of a death knell counting out the years of an ended life. Today the bell tolled for Nashville.

The civilians formed a solemn conclave in the market square. The murmur of voices fell away as the mayor stepped onto the back of a buckboard and raised his arms for silence. The ringing ceased, yet a mournful echo resonated above us. It seemed to me that I could hear the deep, distant drum of Yankee cannon fire in counterpoint as the echo faded. Was it my imagination?

Beside me a young matron burst into tears. The life of proud, independent-minded Tennessee was coming to a close.

The mayor glanced at his pocket watch and removed his top hat in a gesture of regret. "Fellow citizens of Nashville," he began. "We have, this very hour, received word that General John B. Floyd and General Gideon J. Pillow, the ranking Confederate officers at Fort Donelson, have escaped across the Cumberland River with Floyd's Virginia Brigade."

A moan emanated from the packed crowd. I thought of young William among General Grant's boys in blue, storming the gates of Fort Donelson. For the first time in months I felt a surge of hope. If William still lived, he might be as near to me as the sound of artillery!

Again the mayor spread his arms in request for calm and order. His voice cracked with emotion as he addressed us. "General Buckner remains behind to yield Fort Donelson to the Northern aggressors. We are left in the hands of the enemy." An agonized cry of collective grief, terror, and disbelief arose.

"Please!" shouted the mayor. "We must remain calm! Our gallant forces are retreating south across the bridge, and no private citizen will be allowed to cross until the army is over! It must be so! Our boys must remain free to return and fight another day!"

From that hour, a state of confusion reigned in the city. Markets were stormed by the citizenry. Women shouldered great slabs of bacon and rolled barrels of flour down the streets. They gathered up bolts of fabric and clothing enough to supply them and their children for whatever might come. On every block, young Confederate recruits stopped at their homes to kiss wives and sweethearts and mothers farewell.

I withdrew from the chaos to the Brown Hotel and took a room while other guests hurriedly checked out and prepared to follow in the wake of the retreating army. Settling in a chair beside the window, I observed the panic beneath me until night fell. The sky was alight with burning cotton warehouses. In spite of the eerie orange glow, I fell asleep, fully clothed, sometime past midnight.

Several hours later a series of terrible explosions shook the glass in the windowpanes. I woke with a start as three more horrific blasts issued from the direction of the river. I learned later that General Floyd had ordered the strategic destruction of the railroad and suspension bridges over the Cumberland after the retreat of Confederate forces. This action trapped thousands of terrified civilians in the city and in the path of the oncoming Union army.

I splashed water on my face, and without emotion I muttered, "So, the war is over in Nashville. Perhaps, if we are lucky it will all end this quickly."

After that, Nashville was as silent as a tomb. Women, children, and those too old to fight huddled in their houses to await the dreaded arrival of Federal troops. There was nothing for me to do now but remain at my post beside the window to watch for the victorious Army of the Ohio and my son as they paraded down the main thoroughfare before me. I determined that when William passed my way, I would snatch him from the ranks and expose him to his officers as a runaway child! After that I would drag him, hog-tied if necessary, home to his grieving mother and the farm!

———◆———

For a week after the fall of Fort Donelson, Nashville watched for the expected invasion of the dreaded Yankees. To my great disappointment the Federal forces made no attempt to enter the city. I sent a letter to Alcie and the children expressing my hopes that when the Federals did occupy the town, William would be among them.

All the young men of military age in Nashville had gone south with the Confederate army. The mayor and most of the city council remained behind, fuming at the fact that Nashville had been left defenseless. The anticipation of the evil deeds that would unfold when the Yankees came caused that week to be called the Great Panic.

I awoke the morning of the twentieth to the sound of iron-shod horses trotting purposefully across the cobbles of the street. My first thought was that the Yankees had finally arrived from Fort Donelson eighty miles away. I was wrong.

The Confederate forces were on the way to Murfreesboro when it occurred to General Floyd that he had left a mighty heap of supplies back in Nashville. General Nathan Bedford Forrest, with a small detachment of cavalry, was sent to recover the army stores and get them south to the retreating army. I knew this was sure to cause a riot in the city because the people felt they had been promised the stores. What else would they have to live on when the fearsome Yankees took the city?

I ate my breakfast hurriedly as the swell of angry voices grew and a mass of wounded soldiers and citizens of all types swarmed toward the market square and the Confederate warehouses to take possession. Even black slaves were there, ordered by their masters to raid and carry away goods.

Last to arrive on the scene, I hung back as I witnessed Forrest's horsemen surround the crowd.

Forrest, six feet of lean and steely-eyed strength, rose in his stirrups and bellowed, "In the name of the Confederacy! Y'all listen up and git on home! The Confederacy'll have these here supplies to fight the Yankees, and you'll not hinder us from takin' them, neither!" I noted that he spoke with an unschooled tongue. Word was that Old Bedford, as he was called, was looked down on by the majority of Rebel officers because he was not of the gentry. There was wild fury in Forrest's eyes, and I sensed he was dangerous.

One of his troopers shouted, "Git on home now! The general means what he says!"

Forrest enjoined, "I'll have this here square clear in one minute or by the Almighty, you'll be sorry in two!"

The mob remained steadfast, although women who had served the Confederacy these many months suddenly looked at one another in agonized disbelief. Many gathered up their younguns and made ready to run.

Forrest's gruff order went unheeded. The general stared at his pocket watch and raised his hand in preparation for the signal. Some fool civilian fired a shot into the air. At that moment Forrest dropped his hand, and the Confederate cavalry charged into the screaming women and old folks and slaves.

Ducking behind a column of the portico, only

twenty-five yards from the line of action, I watched as Forrest's men rode down a group of slaves among the population. Rifle butts raised and slammed down, and the cries of the fallen were drowned out by the curses of the soldiers.

The incident was over in less than five minutes. The square was cleared of all except for two dozen colored men and women who had been injured too badly to walk or killed outright.

Sprawled in his own blood near the center of the square was old Samuel Burton, doorman at my hotel. I strode quickly toward him, thinking I would get him home to his quarters.

Samuel was ominously still, and I felt sick at heart. The old man was too fragile to be ridden down and survive. Kneeling beside him, I touched his hand and said his name. He was dead.

The sharp point of a saber pricked the fabric of my coat just between the shoulder blades. I raised my hands.

"Is this nigger yourn?" I recognized the voice of Nathan Bedford Forrest. On his mount, he towered over me.

I managed to control my rage; no doubt on account of the sword. "I don't own a slave, General Forrest."

"You a nigger lover then? A black Republican, ere you? Where you know this here critter from?"

"Samuel is the doorman at my hotel."

"Not no more he ain't. He's rubbish now." Forrest laughed.

Anger rushed through me. "It didn't have to be done this way," I spat.

The blade nudged me harder. "Civil disorder. These here troopers only struck down the rebellious slaves." Forrest laughed in amazement at my concern. "Not one white woman nor child bloodied. Just a mite humbled. And look here. Peace is restored. Don't tell me my business. Now git up off'n yer knees."

He withdrew the sword. I stood and turned to face him, burning his visage into my memory: impatient, deep-set gray eyes, chiseled features, neatly trimmed grizzled spade beard.

"I'll get a wagon and fetch the body back to his home," I said.

"Where would that be?"

"Brown Hotel."

"And what be yore name?"

"Jesse Dodson."

"You're a Tennessean, it's plain by your speech. Where abouts exactly?"

"McMinn, east of the Cumberlands." Even just mentioning the county, I inwardly chided myself for answering so directly. Why was Forrest interested in such details?

He nodded his head and narrowed his eyes in thought. "I know that county. They lynch Yankees over yonder I hear. Blue bellies won't get in there. You got you a good horse?" Forrest was grinning.

"Good enough."

"How about this here body? You got you a buck-board to carry it?"

"I will fetch one."

"Yes. That you will. You will fetch a buckboard and be back here ready to empty out that there warehouse and haul these here supplies where I tell you to. It come to me you ere a mite too big and healthy not to be of some use to the South. You'll make a fine gravedigger. I'll make you boss over a hundred darkies. Consider your-self swore into the army of the Confederacy. Yessir. Private Jesse Dodson. Be back in ten minutes, Private Dodson, or you will think a load of stone just busted loose on your sorry head. Keep in mind I shoot desert-ers." I had no doubt he meant both ends of that equation to be personally taken.

With that, he rode away toward the heap of supplies and the wagons that had been commandeered to haul the goods.

With Old Bedford's warning ringing in my ears, it was all I could do not to sprint to the stable, saddle Trafalger, and make a mad dash out of town. I was a mere ten minutes ahead of Forrest's firing squad. No doubt the General would be watching the time on his gold pocket watch and would indeed kill me if I was not far out of his grasp.

I walked toward the barn behind the hotel. Meeting up with Cyrus, the stableboy, I ordered him in the name of General Forrest to hitch a team of mules to the hotel buck-board. Then I rapidly went to work saddling Trafalger.

Cyrus muttered, "What the bossman gonna say 'bout givin' the buckboard to that Forrest?"

"He would not argue. Now get to it, Cyrus, or we'll all be in hot water."

"Yessuh," he said, and then paused a moment. "That Gen'ral Forrest? I just hear he kill some folk on down to the square."

"That he did," I replied over my shoulder, not wanting to tell him about Samuel.

"Samuel Burton be down in that square."

"Yes." There was no avoiding it.

"When he comin' home?"

"He is not coming home."

The boy's chin trembled. Hands dropped to his side. "Samuel be my granpap. What you mean, suh, he ain't comin'?"

"He's dead."

Now there erupted a wail of grief that I had not anticipated. "Forrest kill my granpap! I'se gonna kill that slaver! I heard 'bout him. He the one what sold half the slaves in Tennessee! Slave trader! Bounty man! I'se gonna kill him like he done Granpap!"

The boy snatched up a pitchfork and was heading toward daylight and death when I mounted Trafalger and loped out to stop him.

"Drop that pitchfork, boy!" I commanded. "Whoa up! You aimin' to get yourself killed? It won't bring your grandpa back."

Ten seconds passed. It seemed like my entire allotted

time. I expected to see Forrest ride around the corner into the stable yard any instant.

"I cain't go nowheres. Mistuh Brown, he put a bounty on my head, shore enuff."

"The Yankees are a'comin'." I grabbed the fork and tossed it away. "There won't be no more bounty for runaways because y'all will be free! Tell you what: Let's us both get away from Old Bedford and his cutthroats."

Cyrus almost smiled. With one backward glance, he latched onto my hand and swung up onto the saddle behind me.

With three minutes to spare, I spurred Trafalger out of the yard.

Clutching me tightly, Cyrus yelled, "Rebs be all 'long this a'way suh! I show you where to ride straight to them Yankees!"

Following the directions of Cyrus, we took a shortcut across the fields toward the outskirts of Nashville.

I dared not look back, although I felt the rage of General Nathan Bedford Forrest following hot on our heels. Trafalger seemed not to notice the extra weight of his burden. He sailed effortlessly over stone walls and split-rail fences. The ease with which 'Falger put distance between us and the Rebels drew admiration from Cyrus.

"Must be a Yankee hoss!" said the boy after several breathless miles. "Run fast as any critter I ever see'd."

I reined Trafalger up under a hickory tree several miles away from Forrest. "My horse don't fancy joinin' up with ex–slave traders pretending to be gentlemen, I reckon."

For the moment we were safe from Bedford Forrest and his gravediggers. I could not imagine the terrible events that waited ahead for me and my family at the hands of General Nathan Bedford Forrest. Had I known the suffering he was to bring into our lives I would have returned that hour to Nashville and shot him out of his saddle.

———⊳◈⊲———

With Cyrus to guide us, we rode out to the suburbs of Edgefield.

Cyrus said, "Yankees mos' likely come this a'way when they comes. Edgefield is the place they be comin' to, suh. Oughta wait here."

Finding a dilapidated and crowded hotel, I was told 'my boy' would have to sleep out of doors. I dared not leave the agitated young man alone after the death of his grandfather. I stabled Trafalger and paid for two sacks of clean straw for Cyrus and me to sleep on in the barn.

I rested uneasily, with visions of Forrest's cavalry charge and of William being trampled by ten thousand horses.

Early Sabbath morning on February 23, I was awakened to the shouts of a large group of children who had been walking through the drizzle to Sunday school.

"It's them!" sounded the alarm. "The Yankees! Oh Mama! It's the Yankees!"

"The Yankees are coming!"

"Run for it! Hide quick! The blue bellies are ridin' in!"

I leaped from the straw as the bell of the Presbyterian church began to clang wildly.

Pulling on my boots and dashing coatless into the street I witnessed frightened women running out to retrieve their children to hide them from the dreaded Federal troopers. Doors on neat frame houses slammed shut with sounds like the crack of rifle fire; window shades were instantly drawn on the ground floors, and moments later the curtains of the upper stories were like-wise closed. The church bell fell silent.

Within a matter of moments I was the only human remaining on the rutted, muddy lane. In the house across the street I saw the corner of a drape lift. Smiling and raising my hand in a wave of acknowledgment, I thought I heard a feminine shriek. The fabric instantly fell back.

Fear was the predominant emotion of the Edgefield townsfolk that Sunday morning. I was certainly the only person in all the area around Nashville who had been looking forward to this moment.

A surge of excitement coursed through me. Would William be among these first Union soldiers? Cold rain penetrated my shirt and gripped my bones, yet I was warmed with hope. William was coming! I waited at the bend in the road and listened to the approach of iron-shod horses.

A troop of Federal horsemen rode up and around me. There were only about fifty of them in all. Their eyes were alert to the rooftops and alleyways, but their rifles were not cocked nor their sabers drawn.

"Excuse me, sir," asked a young lieutenant politely. "Do you know where there is a livery stable?"

I had seen one on our entry into Edgefield, and I directed the officer. "There has been some looting," I said. "Best go gently about what you take."

The lieutenant looked shocked. "We have the strictest orders to treat the citizens with the utmost courtesy," he said. "And to pay for whatever we require . . . in gold."

This was certainly a different slant to the dreaded Yankee invasion.

"Specifically," the young, trim officer continued, "our supplies are still miles back, and we have some mounts in need of a blacksmith's attention and some tack in want of repair. Our company saddler is laid up with the grippe."

"I'm a fair hand at shoeing," I admitted. "And I can stitch leather."

"Well then," the lieutenant agreed. "Would you like employment?"

For the next week I served the Yankees and was paid well for my time. Of the anticipated pillaging, I saw none. Nor was I the only civilian who found the Feder-als to be agreeable taskmasters; many others swallowed their Southern pride after they compared the attitude of the Northerners to what they had seen of Old Bedford. I had plenty of opportunity to inquire after William, but no one had heard tell of him.

When it came time for me to leave and report my failure to Alcie, the lieutenant asked me if I would care to enlist as substitute saddler for their company permanently.

"No, thank you kindly," I responded. "I'm sorry y'all have to go to fightin', but me, I'm goin' home."

Just before leaving Edgefield, Cyrus approached me. "Them bluecoats say I don't gotta go back to Bossman. But if they leaves here, somebody might make me. What should I do, Mistuh Jesse?"

"Cyrus, it seems to me that the Good Lord has provided you a chance to be free. You stay that way. Go farther north if you have to. As you go, you heed how you can say 'thank you' to the Lord for what He has given you, and like the Good Book says, He'll direct your path."

The young man's face came all over serious and thoughtful. "I surely will do that, Mistuh Jesse. I surely will."

CHAPTER 2

⏀ELLICO JUNCTION
MAY 1863

Over a year passed since the fall of Nashville, and still no word of William reached us. Battles raged east, west, and south of us, but around McMinn County in East Tennessee, the war did not seem to exist. The country was foraged over by Rebel troops, but mainly they left things be, and the Yankees stayed away entirely.

I first heard the news about the runaway slaves from R. J. Ferguson, who was owner of Tellico Junction General Store as well as postmaster. Those of us who frequented R. J.'s store shortened the name of the place to Tellico Junk. The title fit the atmosphere. It was well known that in 1790 R. J.'s granddaddy followed Daniel Boone into Tennessee to trade with the Indians and trappers. With the exception of corn liquor, which the old man made in a still out back, nothing much sold. Tellico Punch is what kept the old trade in business in the early days. R. J., the present owner, inherited the establishment before my time. He was a small and rowdy man with the temper of a fighting cock when he sampled too much of his granddaddy's punch. Then he got saved at a Methodist camp meeting and forsook hard liquor of every variety. He destroyed his granddaddy's still and burned the famous and secret family recipe for Tellico Punch the same day. This was a great disappointment to many of the riffraff among the local male population who thought highly of Tellico Punch.

As for all the items that had not sold in the long history of the store, R. J. kept the stuff. It remained where his grandfather had placed it. Though Tennessee was a goodly way from the ocean, a whaler's harpoon and a tangle of sea-fishing nets hung from the rafters. I always supposed that R. J.'s grandfather had crossed the Cumberland Mountains and expected to find the Pacific Ocean, then turned back east in disappointment. Leather knee breeches, powdered wigs, and ladies' garments from the last century were piled in a dusty mound behind other heaps of junk. There was too much to name and all of it useless.

In the center of the room were a half-dozen cracked, desiccated saddles and a conglomeration of decayed bridles. King of the heap was an ancient Mexican saddle that someone had brought home from the war against Santa Anna. Being a saddler and a farrier in my spare time, I considered the Mexican rig to be the only item of interest. Pommel, swells, and cantle were built so high that a man could not be shaken loose and would only fall out if the horse was turned upside down.

There was little of value to be got in R. J.'s store, yet he stayed in business because of the Post Office pigeon-holes in the corner near the fireplace. R. J. received the government contract to deliver the mail shortly after he destroyed the still. He considered this to be a divine reward from the Almighty. For as long as I could remember, R. J. Ferguson dispensed mail, wrote letters for the unlearned, swore affidavits, and witnessed wills from the caged corner. More latterly he had posted casualty lists from the battles.

Although R. J. was technically an employee of the government, he was not in danger from neighbors with Southern sympathies. We all came to Tellico Junk to get our mail and hear the latest news of the war.

Like me, R. J. kept his mouth shut and his thoughts to himself about the follies on both sides of the Mason-Dixon line. Our tiny speck of earth was a parade ground for both causes. Some owned slaves. Many were aboli-tionists. It was rumored that a few in our county had helped contraband slaves escape north into Ohio.

Over the years I had begun to believe that R. J. was a part of the Underground Railroad. More than once I had heard sounds escaping from the trapdoor of his cel-lar. The basement was accessible only by shifting a heap of ladies' corsets off a second stack of barrels.

"Varmints!" R. J. growled on those occasions as he

stamped his hobnailed boot hard on the planks of the floor.

I pretended to pay the stirring no mind. I had noticed, however, that unlike the other petrified stuff in his establishment, the unmentionables of the fair sex were in a little different position each time I came in.

Yet, R. J. avoided taking a stand. He grieved with families who lost sons on both sides. Each faction believed that R. J. Ferguson was one of their number. Curiously, he knew all the verses of "Dixie" and could sing out with the best of them. I suppose he also knew the "Star Spangled Banner," but at that time and place it was unwise to raise that tune.

It is enough to say that he went on doing what he was meant to do and nobody bothered him or Tellico Junk.

He was a wizened old man by 1863, but then I could not remember him being otherwise. His back to the door, he was putting the mail up in the letter boxes and shaking his head all the while. I supposed that one of the envelopes had the mark of the war department giving official notice of the death of some McMinn County son.

"Morning, R. J.," I announced myself.

He did not turn around. "Howdy, Jesse."

"It'll be William's birthday. His eighteenth. His mama thinks he'll send us some word when he comes of age. Anything for us?"

"Nope."

I leaned against the upright timber, ducking my head to avoid the dangling harness. "Any news then?"

"Yep." He continued sorting the delivery. "Big battle up Virginny way. A place called Chancellorsville." He completed his task and turned to face me. The usual twinkle in his faded blue eyes was gone. "What's it all for, I ask ye?" He rubbed his hand across his brow.

I knew he did not mean for me to answer the question. "Casualties?" I asked.

"Seventeen thousand boys in blue."

I shuddered and thought of William; just one boy, but he was mine, and my mind could not picture any other face but his. "So many? Lord have mercy, R. J.! Wounded and killed?"

R. J. grimly glanced up at me. "That's just the first sum. Reckon they ain't counted all the wounded yet. Likely there will be more to die among those fellers. Three days it lasted."

I looked for a place to sit down. There was none. Until this time I had not heard of so many dying all in one place. I remarked bitterly, "Lots of folks'll have something to celebrate. A great victory for the Confederacy."

"There ain't no place in this whole wide country that there ain't some mama gonna be cryin' for her boy. The South lost thirteen thousand. Don't know how many maimed or got shot and dyin' by inches. Don't know how it will all end."

I was suddenly angry at the waste. "When there

aren't any more boys left to die maybe? When everything folks love is torn asunder?"

R. J. put his hand on my arm and lowered his voice although there was no one else around to hear. "There's something else I got to tell you." With his rheumy eyes he studied my face. "Can I trust you, Jesse?"

"Yessir."

"Tuck Ringworth had nine slaves run off last week. Two men, three women, and four babies."

Tuck Ringworth was a captain in the Confederate Cavalry. He had been wounded in the arm and was home on furlough. His farm was nine miles to the south of my place. He had a reputation for cruelty toward his servants.

"I know of him."

"I reckon you do. And you know what he does to runaways." His glance flitted to the stack of corsets. "Law gives Ringworth the right to do whatever he wants. Kill 'em if he takes a mind to."

"They're no use to him dead."

"Crippled they can still work. You've seen it. Hamstring the men. Other things to the women. He's got his soldiers out lookin' for this bunch. Ringworth ain't up to the chase, but there's a number who signed on to his cavalry unit, and they're scouring every hill and valley for contraband."

"Those slaves got to be a far piece off by now."

"Mebbe." He pursed his lips in thought. "Most likely they're still around somewheres. And if'n they was . . ."

"I got a family," I said as a chill went through me. What Tuck Ringworth would do to runaway slaves, he would also cause to be done to those who helped them flee.

"Your farm is the last before the mountains. If'n the contraband was to reach your place, cross your fields . . ."

I knew with certainty that if I nodded my head, R. J.'s runaways would emerge from beneath the corsets and follow me home. Sooner or later doom would also come knocking at my door. And yet, the dead of Chancellorsville urged me to not let their miserable deaths be for no reason.

I replied, "You know my left eye is a bit dim since that accident I had when I was a child. I just can't see out of that side like I used to. Why, a fella could walk all the way through my herd of heifers in my lower field, cross the creek and disappear into the woods, and I'd never know if it was a human or just a cow."

R. J. grinned. "I thought you had that bull down in the lower pasture."

"You mean the one that chased John Dixon and tried to kill him last week?"

"The very one."

"Too dangerous. Kids want to try some fishing down at the creek. I don't want any one of them coming within reach of that bull."

"He's a mean'un!" R. J. agreed.

"Yessir, he is. And that being the case I am planning

on shifting that bull away off to the south pasture. Bringing the heifers in to graze. Tomorrow."

R. J. nodded absently and turned to stare into the letter boxes again. "Right smart of you to think of it. Some child could wander into the bull's territory and something tragical might come of it."

<hr>

That evening, against the wishes of Alcie, I moved Ahab the bull out of the lower pasture.

"That critter is big as a locomotive and will bust through the split-rail fence like it isn't there."

I explained. "Fishing down at the swimming hole is too good this time of year for the neighbors to pass up. Don't want Ahab killing anybody."

"Lord, Jesse! The lower pasture is rock wall on three sides and the crick on the other! Nothing else will hold him."

She was right. Ahab was as mean as they come. When he took a hankering to go visiting, there was not much that could hold him back except in that lower pasture.

I could not explain to Alcie that R. J. was bringing a wagonload of Tuck Ringworth's runaway slaves out to the farm and the only safe way out of the valley was through our lower field and across the creek. With Ahab guarding the crossing, those folks would not have to worry about Tuck catching up to them. Nine humans: women toting babies, old, worn-out menfolk; they would not make it five yards into the field before the bull would run them down.

"Now Alcie, you know there's only one thing that'll keep a bull-critter from wandering. A sweet, little heifer on the straw. That's the trick . . ." I slipped my arm around her waist and tried for a kiss, but she was not interested in testing my theory.

"Nothing so sorrowful as a lonely bull." She grinned at me in a teasing way then grabbed up the milk bucket and headed for the milking stool. "You know how it is. All right, then. Just be sure you leave a sweet, young cow in there to keep him busy."

For good measure and so as not to wear out one cow, I drove two good-natured heifers in with Ahab.

That night, younguns prayed up and tucked in, Alcie reconfirmed my notion about why man-critters give up a wandering life and settle down with one woman. I awoke the next morning convinced that Ahab would not have the will or the energy to break through that flimsy fence.

I was wrong.

Drawing water from the well, I chanced to look up. Ahab's female companions grazed contentedly on the tall grass, but Ahab had taken a notion and was altogether gone. A twenty-five-foot section of rail had been smashed to the ground.

Behind me Alcie remarked in a told-you-so voice, "I warned you. He's a Mormon bull. Even two wives aren't enough."

"Well he's halfway to Zion by now, Alcie."

"Hmmm. I'll have your breakfast waiting when you fetch him back."

I had just led 'Falger to the corral and left our boy Loren in charge of mending the fence when I spotted the dust of R. J.'s freight wagon coming up the lane.

"Howdy, Jesse! Loren!" R. J. bellowed while he was still one hundred yards away.

Surrounded by younguns and with the baby on her hip, Alcie waved and hollered, "Mornin', R. J. I got coffee and biscuits in the warmer if you're hungry."

Alcie always had a fondness for R. J. on account of his burning the recipe for Tellico Punch. Most of the women admired him for making it just that much harder for the menfolk to get their lips on the rim of a jug of hard liquor.

R. J., who was a confirmed bachelor, also had a fondness for Alcie. He often remarked how amazing it was that a woman of Alcie's small size could have such a large litter of kids and not look altogether swaybacked, worn-out, and bedraggled. Mutual fondness aside, I felt it best that Alcie never know about our small part in the aid of Tuck Ringworth's slaves.

I rode out to meet R. J. alone. Coming alongside the wagon I said in a quiet voice, "You got them?"

"Yessir. You mind if I back the wagon into the barn?"

"I never told Alcie about this. Nor the younguns."

He cocked an eyebrow at me. "You never told Alcie?"

"I don't want her in hot water if it should go wrong."

R. J. rubbed his cheek. "I reckon Alcie didn't mention anything like this to you?"

"Why should she?"

R. J. grinned. "Time you know'd. She's the one brought this idea to mind. Told me at church if the railroad was still running . . ."

"Railroad?"

"Indeed. Been called the Underground Railroad for years."

"You mean she's known about all this?"

"You might say that. Your boy William first, then Alcie. Nigh on four years them two been helpin' out." He slapped the lines down on the rumps of the mules. "Things was just fine until you moved that bull down to block the ford of the crick. Alcie know'd you wouldn't move the critter if'n she asked, so she asked me to ask, then argued with you about what a foolish idee t'were to move ol' Ahab. She was right certain if she crossed you about it your stubborn streak would kick in and you'd move the bull for sure."

I was dumbfounded. How long had Alcie been taking the bit in her teeth against my will? And William, too? "I oughta give both of them a good hiding."

"You might do that if'n you ever catch up to

William. I'd think twice about layin' a hand on that woman of yourn. Alcie would take a chunk of stovewood to you if'n you ever tried t' whup her."

He was right. Alcie was prone to doing what was right and figuring I'd find out after the deed was done. "I should've known." I glanced back at the heap of manure in the wagon bed. It stunk. "All of them in there? Under that stuff?"

R. J. winked. "If'n you was, let's say, a Reb officer in a shiny new uniform, an' your sweetheart just stitched on them golden braids an' 'broidered her initials next to your heart . . . would you go a'diggin' through a load of bull manure to find anything a'tall?"

"Babies in there too?"

"They're all nine hid under a false bottom. Got water an' vittles. It ain't so bad. We give the babies a drop of laudanum to keep 'em quiet. Just keep them younguns of yourn out of the barn till nightfall, and no one will ever know."

"My younguns ain't likely to go playing in bull manure."

"I was counting on that. Now, speakin' of bulls, have y'all lost that big bull of yourn?"

"'Deed I did. Broke the fence just like I knew he would. And Alcie said he would. He's gone all right."

"Yep. Well, I seen him back up the road a mile and a half toward Twizick's farm. Best git on and fetch him back, Jesse, or somebody's a'gonna come after y'all for damages."

"Lord," I remarked, bringing 'Falger around and spurring him to the road.

I heard R. J. call, "Hold on! I got somethin' for y'all!"

Too harried to turn back, I hollered, "Leave it with Alcie!"

Trafalger was a fine horse, and his long, easy strides fairly ate up the mile and a half to Twizick's farm. Ahab's tracks mingled with those of two dozen horses, but the busted rails in the Twizicks' fence led me to believe that the search would be a short one.

"He's gone that a'way," I mumbled to 'Falger.

The grass in that pasture was lush; belly high to Trafalger. Ahab had cut a wide swath through it that disappeared into the stand of pine trees at the far side. I could not think why that bull had not stopped to graze a bit.

We loped across the field and heard the bawling of a cow beyond the woods.

"Well, now," I remarked, "Ahab's wasted no time at all. Twizick had had a hankerin' to breed his stock to Ahab. Looks like God answered his prayers."

I figured I'd throw a rope on Twizick's cow and use her as bait to lead Ahab back home.

Entering the thick, dark stand of trees, I paused a moment to listen. The rush of the distant creek and a hushed whisper of wind in the trees nearly drowned out the murmur of men's voices.

I shook my head in defeat. Twizick had found my wandering bull before I had. I hollered, "Howdy, Twizick!

I come to fetch back Ahab! Give a holler so's I can find you!"

Ahab's strong bellow issued from the trees on my right. I remarked to my horse, "He's down at the crick."

There followed the crack of a rifle, then two more. "All right, Twizick!" I shouted. "No need to waste the powder. I got a fix on you!"

'Falger snorted, neighed, and the high whinny of a horse returned to him. I gave him his head, and he took me straight as an arrow into the camp of two dozen Rebel cavalrymen.

Ahab was in the center of the camp, hanging from a stout tree by his hind legs. He was bleeding fresh from a wide slash across his throat, and a lean, hungry-looking soldier was preparing to gut him with his saber.

I said, "That's my prize bull you've slaughtered."

Their picket, a boy of William's age, pointed his carbine at my head.

"This was a stray. Busted through two fences to come to supper. He's the main course. Now raise your hands, mister."

I obeyed, determined to let the matter drop. After all I was outnumbered two dozen to one.

"That ol' bull will feed half the Reb army," I said cheerfully. "You plan to eat him here or wrap him up?"

Their captain replied, "Some of both." He motioned the boy to lower his aim and for me to drop my hands. He cocked an eye at me and shoved his hat back on his head. "You look like a reasonable feller. Got one of them fine East Tennessee horses we come looking for."

Ahab was one thing. Trafalger was another. "You intend to eat him too?"

"Nawsir. We intend to ride him." He sauntered toward me. "Us and General Nathan Bedford Forrest intend to ride him and chase down every blue belly in East Tennessee. You got any objections?"

He reached out to grab the reins. At my cue, Trafalger tossed his head hard, knocking the Reb a staggering blow in the side of his face. The officer reeled back and fell, cursing, on the ground.

Responding to the pressure of my legs and a slight tug on the reins, 'Falger backed out of the camp. "This horse won't be rode by any man but me, fellers. Give my compliments to Old Bedford!"

With shouts and curses ringing out behind us, Trafalger lit out through the thick wood, running a course worthy of the best foxhunt in Tennessee. Only this time we were the fox.

Bullets buzzed past my ears like angry bees. Bark shattered on the impact and stung my face. Following the bank of the creek, I counted on the fact that 'Falger and I had ridden this land a thousand times and the men of Bedford Forrest were strangers here.

At the ford 'Falger charged across without urging. Instinct and fear somehow urged him to a speed and agility that I had never experienced on any horse before that day. He outdistanced the tired mounts of the cavalry, but I could still hear them behind us. They would not give up, no doubt, tracking us back to our own front door unless I could outride and outfox them.

A series of high stone fences was ahead, spaced a mere twenty-five yards apart. Last autumn 'Falger had soared over two of the three chasing a fox when no other horse in the county had managed. The third was in my judgment too high even for 'Falger. I had pulled him up, though he was game to try it. The fox had escaped through a hole.

Today, however, like the fox, there was no way of escape except through the wall or over it.

"They're eating our dust!"

The first barricade loomed ahead of us. Standing at six feet high, my horse took it without hesitation. And so with the second. The Rebs likewise cleared the wall; their yells echoed joyfully through the forest.

The third fence had been built to keep deer out of the corn patch of some long forgotten pioneer. Fifty years had passed and still it stood, solid and insurmountable. I had never measured it; never thought to. No horse had ever jumped it.

But then, 'Falger was no ordinary horse. He was eager to try for it. In his mind the fox who had beat him was still on the other side, and he would run him down! I felt him strain, so I let him go.

"All right then, you've been hankerin'! Take us home!"

At my words, 'Falger seemed to take flight. The

stone loomed in front of my face, and I thought we'd smash it head-on, but we did not! For an instant I felt as if man could truly fly. Up and up we sailed! One moment of rush with wind; the top of the fence beneath my stirrups and we began the descent!

Behind us came the shout of dismay, "He's took the fence!"

I thought we were safe, and then the unthinkable happened: The crack of Trafalger's left hind hoof resounded in the air. There was no mercy in that stone; no weakness, no give. 'Falger hung midair for a moment while I flew out of the saddle and into a brier patch. With a terrified scream, legs churning and finding no purchase, 'Falger crashed down. I narrowly escaped being crushed.

The wind knocked out of me, I could only lie where I had fallen. Trafalger struggled to his feet. As if ashamed by his failure, he towered over my body with his head drooping and the reins dragging.

On the other side of the wall I distinctly heard the Rebs swearing in admiration.

One of them called to me. "You still alive, mister?"

I leaped up. "'Deed I am."

"That flyin' horse of yourn? Didn't kill him, did it?"

"No, sir." I brushed myself off.

"I'm right glad to hear that. Purely a horse to admire."

"'Deed he is!" I replied, running my hand down 'Falger's hock and grimacing at the split in his hoof. The blow had knocked his shoe clean off.

"I'm keepin' this here shoe of his as a memento, mister."

"You do that. That's all of him you'll keep."

The Reb laughed. "I don't reckon there's an easy way around this here wall?"

"Not a'horseback. It'll take y'all a few hours out of your way and then my bull will be too rotten to eat."

"Well, then. You win this one, mister. We'll drink a toast to you and Pegasus at our regimental wingding."

"Greet General Forrest for me." I said this cheerfully although a sense of dread settled over me at the thought of Nathan Bedford Forrest in my own county. Would Old Bedford remember the man from McMinn County who deserted him in Nashville a little over a year before?

For the moment, at least, we were free to go. It would have been easy enough for those soldiers to scale the wall and shoot me dead. They had a keen sense of chivalry, and Trafalger had made a good enough fight that they were content to eat my beef and leave the rest alone.

I could not have known that soon I would meet the troops of Bedford Forrest and that there would be no quarter given.

On that day, however, I felt the satisfaction of a fox who had outrun the hounds. In the off chance the Rebs might change their minds, I led Trafalger a dozen different directions and doubled back through the river three times.

There was, at the end of the day, only one regret:

Trafalger had been badly lamed by the stone wall. I would not be riding him for some time.

◆◇◆

It was near midnight when Trafalger and I came limping home. The light of a single candle shone through the window of our farmhouse.

"Alcie!" I called.

She fairly flew out the door and ran to embrace me. "Oh, Jesse! I thought they'd done you in!" She was weeping; her tears dampened my shirt.

"R. J. came back for his wagon 'round suppertime. He said Twizick told him the Johnny Rebs had killed the old bull and chased you across the country! Oh, Jesse! I thought you were dead or taken too! Not two in one day! Dear Lord! Not two!"

"'Falger is lamed. They never laid a hand on me." I tried to comfort her, too weary from the day to comprehend exactly what she had said.

"William's gone, Jesse!"

"Well, yes, Alcie. He'll come back though."

"The letter! The letter! I could not have lived if they had taken you too!"

And now the dim light in my brain began to glow a little brighter. Had not R. J. told me he had something for me? And had I not told him to give it to Alcie? Had the letter from William, or about him, finally arrived?

"Letter," I repeated the word dully. Alcie leaned

heavily against me and sobbed harder. I managed to gather my wits. "Is it about William, then?"

She merely nodded in reply.

I muttered, "'Falger's been lamed. Go inside and get my supper. I'll tend to my horse and be in directly."

A sense of dread filled me as I led the horse into the barn. So the news we had been dreading had come at last. I did not need to see ink on a paper to know. The details were of little consequence. Perhaps the how of it would be explained, but I would never understand the why of it all. R. J.'s freight wagon was gone. I figured that meant the slaves were gone. Their freedom had cost me a bull and the soundness of my horse. Those things meant nothing to me. But the freedom of all their kind had most likely cost the life of my son and a million others. That night I cursed their freedom! Were a million slaves worth the life of my boy?

I fed and watered Trafalger. I did not have the strength to see to his hoof, although any other time it would have been the most urgent need I attended to.

Alcie was sitting by the fire. The glow of its light seemed to drain her face of all color. Exhausted, she stared blankly into the flames.

My plate was heaped with food. The letter was beside it. I washed my hands and sat down as if I intended to eat, but I could not.

The scrawl on the envelope was not in the hand of William. I took out the paper. There were two letters. The first was a brief note of explanation:

Dear Mr. and Mrs. Dodson,

I was with your boy Billy from the first day of our enlistment until the day he was lost to the Rebs at Chancellorsville. He called himself Billy Dearson, but I see from his letter to you it ain't. He were a good friend, and I shall miss him. He were a good soldier, too, and done the Union proud. I reckon by this time you have got word from the War Department that he is gone missing and figgered to be dead by those of us who seen him and the others go down. They was surrounded on top of a ridge and cut off. Them Rebs come a'screaming and fell on him. We was out of cartiges. So was the Rebs, but it was hand to hand and they was more hands than we. Twenty-five or thirty 'gainst him and two others. Only three of us in the mess got out of that scrape. I am sorry it has happened. We could not get back to bury them. A lot of good boys died there. Here is the letter Billy ast I send to you if he was to die. Since he is most likely ded, I am sending it. Captain come and took his belongings and will send them along home. Billy often spoke right kindly of his mother. When he mentioned her cooking it always made us boys in the mess hungry.

Yours truely,
J.S. Hildebrandt, Private

"Alcie?" I was shaking. My strength drained from me. I could not pick up William's letter to read his last words to us.

"They called him Billy," she whispered. "He hated it when I called him Billy."

"I asked in every camp of the Federals for William Dodson. Look here at the letter from his friend. Dearson, he spelled it. No wonder I could not find him."

Alcie kept her gaze locked on the fire. "Right I think that he called himself dear son, since he was, indeed. Don't you think, Jesse?"

I managed to swallow; managed to make myself speak. "This feller didn't see the boy killed. Didn't see him fall! I . . . I won't read his letter of farewell to me until I know!"

Now she turned her pitying eyes on me. "Read it."

Suddenly angry, I scraped my chair back and left the house, slamming the door behind me.

I walked out onto the lane, not knowing where I was going or why. The stars made a soft glowing against the moonless sky. It had been a long time since I had paused to look at creation and pray. My conversations with the Almighty were mundane and businesslike: "When'll it rain? God, we need rain."

Ah, but that night, my heart broke open as the heart of a father will do when his son is lost or dead. I fell to my knees in the dust of the road and cried out to the Almighty in my anguish.

"Is my dear son dead, Lord? Have You taken him

from us forever?" I begged God for a different outcome to the tragedy. I asked God to take my life if William was still alive and in some Rebel prison somewhere. "Take me, but do not let my boy die before he has lived!" I had resisted the battle, and my son, in his good conscience, had taken my place in the line. He was most likely dead, but through that terrible night I could not accept it.

I cannot say what time it was when I crept up to bed. Alcie was asleep. At least she was quiet and still. My soul still churned inside me.

The Rebs had killed my boy or taken him prisoner. At last this was my battle. At last the Confederacy had given me cause to fight.

———⟫◈⟪———

Next morning, Trafalger stood patiently as I tapped the last nail through the horseshoe. The force with which he had struck his right hind hoof against the stone wall had cracked the exterior laminate. The split extended nearly halfway up to the corona band at the top of the foot. The damage was deep and potentially dangerous, but with the special iron shoe I had concocted I figured Trafalger would eventually heal.

Loren, our second son, manning the bellows of my forge, peered down with concern. "Will he heal up right, Father?"

I rasped the front edge of the hoof until it was perfectly

protected by the iron shoe. "He won't be rode for a while. It'll take most of a year before I'll be hunting on him again, I reckon. But this rim we built into the shoe will keep the split from getting worse."

It is strange to say, now, but I was almost grateful for the accident that had lamed Trafalger. Such obvious injury meant that I would not be riding him for a long while, but it was also a certainty that no band of Rebel Cavalry nor Yankee troops passing through our farm would be inclined to confiscate my horse.

This same thought had also entered Loren's head. The image of Trafalger and me outrunning the band of secesh cavalry pleased the boy.

He stroked the muscled shoulder of the big chestnut. "We won't need to hide him from the Rebs no more, will we, Father?"

"Nor from Union foragers neither." I finished the job and straightened slowly. My back still ached some from the fall I had taken.

"And Trafalger will be well by the time this war is over."

I nodded. "We'll hope our boys are all home long before Trafalger is fit to ride."

We both fell silent then, and I supposed that Loren was thinking of William the same as I was. We stood listening to the hum of flies and the swish of Trafalger's tail.

"Wish I knew," Loren said, looking at the horse, but not at me.

I replied in a cheerful, offhanded way, as if I had not discerned his real thoughts. "'Falger's fine and fit. No use to fret over him."

"Wasn't." Loren's face clouded. "I was . . . well . . . wondering about William coming home. Wondering if he was alive."

I lowered my eyes, and, without answering, turned my back on Loren and set my hand to cleaning up. Gruffly, I ordered, "Don't let your mother hear you talk that way. Now take 'Falger back to his stall. Make sure the floor is mucked out. It's your job to keep it clean as your mama's kitchen. Nothing worse for a cracked hoof than standing in filth. Sure way to give him an abscess, and then we'll have to shoot him."

I wish now I would have controlled the grief and anger I felt myself long enough to help Loren deal with the news of his brother. Loren needed to talk about it, and I was no comfort at all. Nor was I any consolation to Alcie or the little ones. I pondered on where he might be and what he would be doing and what I must do to find him again.

Over the past months there had been dark moments, times when I saw the grief in Alcie's eyes, and I went outside and cursed William for doing this to his mother and his brothers and sisters. I had been bitter against him for the torment he had left us with. Yet now I would have to leave my dear family behind while I joined the fight where William had left off.

That evening over supper Alcie spoke about William

to the little ones, who listened to tales about their big brother with wide and awestruck eyes. Louisa and Loren joined in with their mother, but the others, Harriett, Howard, Robert, and tiny Sarah, were too little to remember William at all.

As for me, I ate without speaking. A knot like a fist formed in my gut, and it was all I could do to sit through the conversation.

At last I broke in with a voice that boomed like a cannon, though I had not meant to speak so harshly. "There'll be no more talk about him! It was a cruel and rebellious thing he's done, going off to this war, and now he's left me no choice!"

Alcie's eyes brimmed. "But Jesse," she protested. "It's William's birthday today. Can we not remember what life was for us before?"

"What's the use of it? Everything has changed for us now."

Alcie and Louisa began to weep.

I spat, "See there, Louisa? Look how William has broke your mother's heart."

The little ones, without knowing what the ruckus was about, added their wails to the scene. Loren sat pale and rigid in his seat and glared at me as if I alone was the cause of all misery.

I rose abruptly and went out to check Trafalger's newly shod hoof. It did not require attention, but I needed a little peace. I did not go back to the house until

Alcie, in her nightdress and a shawl, and carrying a pillow and blankets, came out to fetch me.

"Are you coming to bed?" she asked in a gentle, pitying tone like I was one of the younguns and had fallen and scraped my knee. "Or shall I make you a bed in the straw so you can sleep next to 'Falger?"

My back was to her. I brooded against the gate of the stall and could not meet her gaze. I felt ashamed, indignant, and somehow wronged all at the same moment. "'Falger's company suits me. He does not think me a villain."

"Nor do the children."

"And you?"

"You are as comfortable and kindly to me as an old shoe, Jesse Dodson. I do not sleep well without you." She wrapped her arms around me and pressed herself against my back. Her warmth, her softness stirred me, and I turned to embrace her. She was my friend, my love, the only other one who knew what I was feeling.

"Before he ran away . . . was I too harsh with William? Is that why he left?"

"You know he would have joined up when he came of age, no matter what you said."

"We've been grieving nigh onto two years, Alcie."

"You hide your sorrow behind a wall of anger like you hide that horse of yours from the cavalry."

For the first time since I found his bed empty and

knew he had left us I admitted, "I miss my little boy, Alcie."

Alcie sighed and buried her face against my chest. "It's been a long while since he was little. He never even knew he had a new baby sister. Don't even know about little Sarah."

"Don't speak of him as if he's gone forever. It breaks me to think I left so much unsaid to him." My heart became tender, and for the first time tears streamed down my cheeks.

"You're leaving home soon, aren't you, Jesse?"

I nodded slowly. "It's my war now. If William is dead I cannot let his death go for naught. If he lives, then God help me, I'll find him!"

"Give me a few days. There's mending to do. You'll be gone a while I reckon. It's summer now, but you'll need your long handles come autumn. And there are things you'll need to tell the children. Parts of your heart you'll need to leave behind for them to cherish."

"It can't go on long."

"Even a day parted from you is too long. But the hardship for you is the fighting. For me it is being left behind. We will both be strong."

I kissed her and blessed her for knowing me so well. We made our bed up in the straw and passed the night talking about the first night after William was born. We were not more than children ourselves. I was eighteen and Alcie but sixteen.

Alcie said, "William is the same age now as you were when we made him."

"I imagined myself to be a man."

"I lay beside you and watched you sleep and never felt such love. I thought I'd break for loving you so strong."

"I supposed I was capable of accomplishing anything."

Alcie stroked my hair, and I did not feel any different than I had those many years ago.

"When you find him tell him you were exactly his age when he was born. You were man enough to have a family and raise your children to stand up for what they believe in."

"I reckon that is so," I answered quietly as the bitterness left me and something else rushed into my heart. "I am proud of him. I just . . . didn't want him to run off and get himself killed in Mister Lincoln's army. When I held him in my arms the first time . . . I never prayed so hard or feared so much or had so much hope. Easier for me to give up my life than to lose that boy."

"He is so like you."

"He's a better man than me, I fear."

"I never saw two better men, nor two more alike. Stubborn, strong, fierce for the truth. Both of you. What would you have done at his age?"

"I reckon I would've fetched my rifle and gone to join up."

She buried her face against my chest. "Promise me you'll come back, Jesse. Promise me, and I'll believe you no matter what comes."

"How can I make such a vow?"

"Say it, and it will be true. Say it, and God will help you keep your word."

"God help me! I will come home to you, my Alcie girl! And I'll bring the boy back with me if I can!" I kissed her lips, and we wept together.

All too soon I waved good-bye and again traversed the Cumberland Mountains. I knew when I set out that once I wore the blue it might be a powerful long time before I could go home again. What I did not know was what a powerful change would be wrought in me by the crossing.

CHAPTER 3

CAMP SPEAR I
JUNE 1863

It was on the twenty-fifth of May that I went up to Nashville to enlist. Given my frame of mind, I was prepared to join up with the first bunch of boys that looked full of pepper and ready to scrap, be they artillery or foot soldiers. Fortunately for me, before such a thing could befall me, I was hailed in the street by Melvin Long.

He was all kitted up, from the jaunty angle of his cap to the polished scabbard of his saber. His face split in a grin so wide that he like to dropped his pipe. "So, Jesse," he said, remarking the determined set to my jaw. "You've finally had a bellyful and ready to lick yore weight in wildcats."

"Came to enlist," I acknowledged.

"Got an opening for a saddler in our outfit," he said. "You being handy with harness and such and a farrier besides, Cap'n Briant'll be real glad to get even so old a bird as you."

"What do you mean old?" I challenged, ready to give

it right back to him. "Are you calling yourself an infant? I'm thirty-six. You must be most thirty yourself!"

"Twenty-five," he corrected, "and most of the fellers are not above twenty-one. But don't take offense old hoss; you'll add seasoning to the meat." With that he clapped me on the back and led me off to the City Hall to meet Captain Joshua Briant.

Which chance encounter explains how I came to be part of Company F, Third Regiment, Tennessee Volunteer Cavalry. The regiment had been formed some time back. When brand-spanking new they had guarded the trains from Nashville to Murfreesboro. Later on, they got bloodied at the affair at Stones River. Now they were at Camp Spear, just outside Nashville.

Captain Briant was a fine, tall man, three inches above my five-foot-eleven-inch stature. He affected bushy side-whiskers, but he was no dandy for all that. His wide-set green eyes studied me the way I examined a horse or mule that I was considering. "For saddler, is it?" he inquired at last. "You'll get no special consideration for that, Dodson. In this outfit, everyone drills and everyone fights, from the blacksmith to the colonel's servant."

"Yessir," I said. "If it wasn't that way I would be looking somewheres else."

"Bit above the age to be playing at war, aren't you?" He was all of twenty-two. I was getting a mite tired of being regarded as nudging Methuselah, and I said so. The captain ignored my reply and continued, "Or is it that you've heard the draft is coming and you want to avoid being conscripted as a foot soldier? There are other regiments, newly forming of all green troops. Why should we have to break you into our way of doing things?"

"Captain," I said, a little more forcefully than I intended; I came near to calling him Sonny. "I can ride to hounds, I can shoot, I can keep tack in trim, and I can doctor horses . . . but what I came here for is to fight. If that isn't what you are about, I'll thank you to excuse me so I can get on about my business."

To my right, Melvin Long made a strangled noise like he had sucked a gob of tobacco juice up from his pipe.

Briant nodded thoughtfully, and then said, "Ask me what happened to our last saddler."

"All right," I obliged, even though I had a pretty good guess. "I'll bite."

"He was killed on patrol . . . shot right out of the saddle by a sharpshooter he never even saw."

"Captain, do you suppose that Johnny Reb picked him off because he was the saddler? You got a job you want done, and I want to get into this fight . . . what else do we need to discuss?"

Standing up from his desk, Captain Briant extended his hand and shook mine. Then he addressed Long, who had stood silent through the whole exchange. Melvin probably wondered if announcing his friendship with someone who would back talk the captain was such a good idea. "Private Long," Briant said, "thank you for bringing this man to my attention. He will no doubt be a valuable addition to the regiment. Would you please take him to see the surgeon for examination and then to Sergeant Cate for mustering in?"

Long snapped a salute and led me away. On the way to the doctor's tent he kept saying, "Just don't talk like that to the colonel . . . just don't understand . . ."

———⟫◆⟪———

Melvin took me to the office of the regimental surgeon, a man known as Dr. Souers. His name squared well with his preferred treatment, as Melvin told me that Souers prescribed quinine for every complaint from camp fever to piles. Melvin said he'd be back for me and left me in the good doctor's clutches.

Souers was a pig-eyed, flush-faced man, whose breath bore more traces of oh-be-joyful than of quinine. Almost the instant I met him, I wished he was in the market for a horse and I had one to sell; he was that eager to conclude his dealings with me. The entire exam consisted of him looking at my tongue and the soles of my feet. Then he stamped my papers "Approved" and signed his name. "Don't you want to thump my chest or take my temperature or something?" I asked.

"What for?" he said with a dismissing wave of his hand. "You ain't ailin', are you?"

I reflected that any worry I had felt over the vision in

my left eye had been wasted. My sight on that side was blurred some, on account of getting hot lead splashed in it when I was younger. But that was not the eye I aimed with when shooting, and I had been all prepared to argue the point; it was just not necessary.

The next of my new comrades-in-arms was Sergeant Cate, who seemed to be of an age with me. Cate, having heard the report of my interview with the captain, squinted at the surgeon's paper. Then the figure with the three yellow chevrons on his sleeves spat a stream of tobacco juice and wiped his drooping moustache. "Company F," he stated, "is my bailiwick, do ya see? You jump when I holler, don't squat 'less I say to, and if you got something to say, you tell me. Don't be bothering the captain or Lieutenant Freel, and we'll get by. You don't look like an infant to need wet-nursing."

"No, indeed," I concluded.

"Well, then," Sergeant Cate said. "Sign or make your mark here." On a camp stool was a book open to a page that read Company Muster-In Roll, on which I inscribed my name, age, and description. "Got a horse?" Cate asked.

"No, sir," I said. "My family needs all the stock on the farm."

"No matter." Cate shrugged. "If you did, then the army makes note of its value, case it gets shot from under you. And don't be callin' me sir. You say 'Yes, Sergeant,' or 'No, Sergeant.' 'Sir' is only for the buckos with the shoulder straps. Got a firearm?"

"Colt Navy thirty-six," I said, unwrapping and passing him the revolver, butt first.

"Hit anything with it?" he inquired.

"Been known to," I admitted.

"Younger recruits turn up with great horse pistols and no sense. I hafta take 'em away before they go hurtin' themselves or somebody else. Be like you can keep yours. Just don't wear it till I say."

"Yes, Sergeant."

"Saddler you're replacing already messed in with your friend Long, so you can just take his spot in the same tent. That's all."

I must have looked expectant or something, because Sergeant Cate asked, "You forget something?"

"Don't you have to swear me in or like that?"

"Signed is sworn," he remarked. "You're as in as you can get. Draw your uniform and equipage. Oh, and Dodson? Don't be leaving the post without permission."

Melvin Long took me to see the quartermaster sergeant. From him I drew a too-large blouse, too-tight pants, cap and boots that fit, a blanket, a gum poncho, and a cloth haversack. Then Melvin led me to our quarters.

My new home was a Sibley tent. These cone-shaped canvas affairs, designed to house twelve men, covered the field at Camp Spear so as to resemble a Red Indian village. The Third Regiment occupied seventy or so of those tents, and we were not the only outfit stationed there.

Melvin Long smirked at me and remarked, "New man has to sleep nearest the flap," he said.

"From your canary-eatin' grin, that must be bad."

"Maybe not if you don't mind having the duty corporal stomp on your face every two hours all night when he relieves the watch."

I stowed my little sack of personal belongings in the tent, and then a bugle sounded. "What's that mean?"

"That's one you'll learn quick enough," Melvin said. "Chow call."

―――――――⫸◆⫷―――――――

The hours of my first evening in Camp Spear passed in a blur. Meeting many of the hundred or so members of my company, watering and stabling horses and twice standing in rank for no apparent reason, made it hard for me to sort out details. I do recall seeing the lights in hundreds of tents wink out just as the last notes of a mournful bugle call died away. The last sound of all was a drummer boy striking six slow taps on his drum.

I slid into slumber thinking of home . . . Alcie and the children. Then I thought again of William and wondered if he was in a tent like the one I occupied. It made me feel closer to him somehow and reassured me that I was doing the right thing.

Despite Melvin Long's warning about the dangerous position I occupied in the tent, I did not awaken all night. If a corporal stepped on my face, I must not have noticed.

From years of before-dawn chores on the farm, I awoke ahead of daylight without anyone telling me to. Such was not the case for my comrades. Another bugle call sounded, this one strident and demanding, and the men began to groan and mumble to themselves. Then a corporal flung open the tent flap and shouted, "Turn out, you men! All out! Ten minutes to roll call. Shake a leg!"

Since I had slept in my britches and socks like I saw the other veterans do, I had only to pull on my blouse and boots. Then I stood up.

The man sleeping next to me opened one eye and muttered, "Kill the bugler . . . no, kill that corporal first, then the bugler. What time is it anyway?"

"Coming five," I judged, sighting the morning star. "There is no such hour," my drowsy friend grunted, turning and pulling the blanket over his head. By this I judged him to be city folk.

On his way out the door, Melvin Long aimed a kick at the fellow's backside. "Get up, Cochran," Long demanded, "or it'll be your last hour. This mess will not pull extra duty just so's you can get your beauty sleep."

"Go away," Cochran muttered. "You ain't my mother, nor a sergeant neither. I . . . hey, what're you doing?" True to his word, Long was determined that our mess would not be in trouble; and he dragged Cochran upright by a handful of long, greasy hair. "Ow! Hey, that hurts! Let me go!"

"Soon as you're in rank where you belong. Come on here, Jesse. You too, Dobbs. Lend a hand. There, you see," he concluded as another bugle call sounded. "There's assembly already."

Dobbs, an eager, lanky youth who seemed to be all willowy limbs and no body, helped me drag and carry Cochran out to line up facing the great, cleared square surrounded by tents. Cochran grumbled and slouched, but caught Long's baleful stare and remained in line— barefooted and half-clothed, but present.

I noted in the assembled ranks that there were others like Cochran, though most were dressed and presentable. Sergeant Cate called the roll, noted absences of which there were a few, and made his report to the orderly sergeant. Then we were dismissed.

Cochran headed straight back toward the tent, no doubt to resume his interrupted rest, but another bugle call rang out and Long announced, "Stable call. Let's go!"

It was the policy in mounted outfits to care for the stock before breakfast for the men. As Sergeant Cate frequently reminded us, it took sound, sturdy horses to make a cavalry unit, but the monkeys who sat in the saddles were not special at all. Each of us had three horses to lead out to water, then curry and groom, while the animals munched their morning rations.

Cochran hailed me from the next stall over, just as I

was finishing. "Say, Dodson, you seem to know your way around these critters. How do you get them to hold up their feet for you?"

I joined him next to a big bay gelding. "They don't hold them up for you, you have to pick them up," I said, snorting at the ignorance of the city-bred. "Look here," I instructed, squeezing the bay's fetlock. The horse obediently hoisted his leg and let me cradle it behind my knee while I used my pick to clean the sole. "See how easy it is?" I asked.

"I'm not sure," Cochran disagreed. "Let me watch another one."

On our way to mess, Dobbs tagged along beside me, his legs and arms going all different directions as if he had more joints than most folks. "Watch out for Cochran," he warned. "He's a *beat* . . . always trying to get you to do his chores."

"Here, Dobbs," Corporal Pym called after him. "Come back here and stow this rake away properly."

Dobbs obligingly gamboled back toward the stable, but he accidentally trod on the tines of the rake. The handle flipped up, but rather than hitting himself in the face, Dobbs succeeded in knocking the corporal's cap off. Corporal Pym emitted such a stream of oaths that I looked to see the paint peel off the stable wall. But Dobbs was such a good-natured critter that he seemed to take no notice.

——◄◦►——

The month that followed my enlistment was, as promised by Sergeant Cate, one of drill, drill, and more drill. The hours from breakfast till noon were filled with mounted drill with sabers, dismounted drill with carbines, wheels and pivots by company and such. After our noon meal it was regimental maneuvers, with close on a thousand mounted men swinging in lines, columns, and flanking movements.

In the twilight, when the last stable call had been performed and the evening meal was under way, the talk turned to the progress of the war in the places where it was really being fought. "I hear Vicksburg is about played out," Melvin Long said, referring to the Union siege of that city on the Mississippi. He took a pair of hardtack biscuits from the salted water in which they were softening and slapped them into a pan of sizzling pork fat to brown. "It won't be long now before Old Man River is true blue Union from Minnesota to the Gulf."

Many were of the opinion that Robert E. Lee, the Confederate general, would be up to something before he would let that happen. "You watch," Sergeant Cate said. "Massa Bobby Lee will be tryin' something to take the pressure off Vicksburg. Here, put some pepper on that skilligalee."

"Try something where?" Cochran asked.

"North, maybe, like around behind Washington. They say that the Reb General, Longstreet, is on the move."

"And what about us?" I inquired as I labored over a broken bridle. Recruits were always so hard on equipment that I was kept busy repairing tack whenever I was not obliged to drill. "What do you figure for hereabouts?"

Cate nodded gravely before answering, giving his one-word opinion as an old campaigner: "Forrest."

The Confederate chief of the army occupying the southern portion of Middle Tennessee was Braxton Bragg, but when the talk turned to the enemy, the figure most often raised was that persistent devil, my old nemesis, Confederate Cavalry Commander General Nathan Bedford Forrest.

Since Nashville had been retaken from the Rebs back in February of '62, Middle Tennessee was divided between the two opposing armies. We Federals held a line below Nashville that ran southeast from Franklin to Murfreesboro. The secesh faced off with us no more than a dozen miles away, along the line of the Duck River. There had been probes, reconnoiters, and even pitched battles, but no significant changes in position.

Except for Forrest.

Old Bedford was as apt to turn up behind our lines as he was to raid forts on the Mississippi or strike into Kentucky, all of which he had done.

"So you figure Forrest will be coming this way again soon?" I pressed. "He hasn't been heard of for a month."

Cate nodded. "I can smell him, sure as you're born.

But we're ready for him this time. We'll nail his hide to the barn, certain. It's our duty. Yes, indeed, our duty."

I wished I was as confident. For two years Union commanders had chased Old Bedford all over the state without ever pinning him down. He knew when to fight, right enough, and he knew when to withdraw. Three times that I heard tell of his force had been reported "decimated and scattered," only to have him attack again in a week, none the worse for wear.

All of which masked the cause of my personal great grief: If we could not dislodge Forrest and the rest of the Rebs from Middle Tennessee, then there was not even any talk of kicking them out back of the Cumberlands where my home was.

"Yessir," Cate repeated. "I can sure smell him, old slave trader that he is. But we'll bloody his nose right enough this time. Pour me some more of that coffee, Dobbs, and don't spill it on my hand this time."

CHAPTER 4

ULLAHOMA
LATE JUNE 1863

Well before dawn the next day, the twenty-fourth of June, the bugles tore apart my dreams of Alcie and home. No reveille or stable-call either, this sudden blaring of brass horns. The buglers of all twelve companies of our regiment and a like number of infantry and four batteries of artillery all commenced their calls to arms.

"Wake up, Cochran," I said, nudging the man next to me. "It's boots and saddles."

The sudden appearance of Sergeant Cate confirmed the alarm. "Turn out on the double, you men. We're going into action. Corporal Pym, have the men draw rations for three days, forty cartridges apiece, and be ready to move out in fifteen minutes."

Such was the effect of the constant drilling over the previous month that instead of half-sleeping men falling over their nightdresses, we were actually standing to horse in the required quarter hour. In that span we had dressed, watered and saddled our mounts, and received three pounds of hardtack and two of salt pork and twoscore rounds of ammunition.

At the cry, "Company . . . mount!" I swung aboard the tall black gelding I was allotted, and we trotted out of Camp Spear in columns of twos. Until that moment, I had not even had time enough to wonder what the cause of this alarm was or where we were headed.

Three miles south of Nashville, General Stanley, commanding the entire cavalry corps, drew us aside into a cleared field and passed the word. "The whole army is moving south," he said. "General Rosecrans is going to run Bragg and the Rebs out of Shelbyville. Our job is to find Forrest, and after we find him, to back him into a corner and kick the living daylights out of him. What do you say, men?"

We gave him three cheers and a tiger and three more for Rosy Rosecrans as we moved off south again, along the Murfreesboro road. Cate rode by, and as he did so, he wheeled his bald-faced bay alongside my horse. "You will admit I almost had the right of it," he prompted. "It's just that we are not waiting for Old Bedford to move; we're going out after him!"

<hr />

It rained that day and all the next. The Third Regiment scouted ahead of the army and Company F was the vanguard. We did not have the struggles with the mud as did the artillery and the doughfoot soldiers who came after us, but it was mighty lonely way out front.

On the morning of the twenty-seventh, we busted through Guy's Gap and got the word that Bragg had not even waited for our coming but had withdrawn the Confederate troops away south toward Tullahoma. Seems he saw that Rosy's strategy of encirclement was about to work, and Bragg wanted no part of it. Of Forrest, there was no word at all.

That was the day on which I had my first encounter with the Rebs in battle.

Our company was spread out in skirmish lines, in widely spaced ranks of sixteen men across. As chance would have it, my messmates and I were in the first rank, with Dobbs, Cochran, Long, and me to the extreme left of the boggy trace. We advanced at a deliberate gait, aware that we should be encountering the Reb rear guard at any time.

"Jesse," Dobbs sang out, "I see something moving up ahead."

As he spoke the words there came the dry rattle of musket fire and a lead hornet buzzed past my left ear. "Have at 'em, boys," Long shouted. "This is what we came for!"

With that our side of the line surged forward, across a swollen creekbed and up a brushy hillside. I caught a glimpse of a gray-clad figure drawing down on me from behind a fallen log. He looked the age of my son,

William, and it surely did give me pause. Then the spell was broken, and we both fired and both missed. Then as he had only a single-shot weapon and no time to reload, he turned and skedaddled up the slope.

All of my comrades had similar experiences driving in the Confederate pickets, and we all burst into a clearing on the hillside at about the same time. Long was hollering like crazy, and Cochran had a big grin on his face as if we were about to win the war right there.

Then across the intervening space of thirty yards of open ground we heard a voice shout, "Front rank . . . fire!" The shadows under the limbs of a grove of black cherries exploded with the roar of mass rifle fire, and the view ahead disappeared in a cloud of smoke.

I heard Cochran yell, "I'm hit!" but had no time to spare him a thought right then, since my horse screamed and pitched forward at that same instant. I let go of the reins so as to vault clear of the gelding as he tumbled, but my Sharps carbine pivoted on its strap, and the butt clobbered me in the back of the head. I ended up under the neck of the fallen critter, on the downhill angle. The muzzle of my weapon plunged six inches deep in mud. I could not have fought back, even had I been in a position to do so.

Long, Cochran, and Dobbs wheeled for the cover of the brush through which we had come and our bugle sounded recall. I would gladly have obliged, but the black horse was stone dead. What was more, exposed as I was on the open hillside, only the carcass lying between me and the Rebs kept me from getting my own share of minié balls.

As soon as I recovered my scattered wits, I crawled backward down the slope, hiding from view as best I could behind my fallen mount. Whether the secesh could see me or if they just guessed at my whereabouts, I kept hearing musket fire and seeing the jerk of the dead horse's body as the heavy slugs slammed into it.

Sergeant Cate grabbed me by the leg and pulled me down into a gully. I tried to thank him, but he shut me up by telling me what a fool I was and using other, more colorful descriptions. "Our job is to scout the enemy dispositions and report back," he said. "You can't report back if you're dead, Dodson. There'll be no more charging unless you get the order, understand? I expected more control from an older man." He was right, of course. I had come near to getting myself killed my first time under fire and to no purpose whatsoever. "Drop back and see if you can pick up another mount," Cate ordered. "And when you come back, be ready to do a job, not be a hero."

I caught a spare horse from Company D. Seems one of their troopers had taken a ball on the point of his knee. He was out of the fight and out of the war and more than likely going to be shy a leg.

When I rode to rejoin my outfit, I glanced down at my own uninjured shin. There, streaking the shoulder of the dun-colored horse was a fan-shaped stain of blood, right where the former rider's leg had been.

Cochran's wound was no more than a scratch along the line of his jawbone. It came to me soon as I saw it that the scrape could have been made by a tree branch same as a musket ball, but to Cochran it was almost mortal. "Come near taking my head clean off," he told everyone who would listen. "I gotta get me to an aid station."

Sergeant Cate disabused him of that notion right away. The sergeant slapped a handful of stinging, camphorated goo on the place. When Cochran yelped like a scalded pup, the sergeant told him to get back in ranks or he would smear the gunk around some more.

The report from the right side of our line was of greater importance than what my group had discovered. Tullahoma was ahead, on a plateau. The single wagon-width track that led up there was covered by a battery of Confederate cannon, just waiting for our troops to march up the defile. It was our job to root them out, if we could, so as not to delay the passage of the infantry. We posted pickets on our end to watch out for a Reb flanking maneuver, then the rest of Company F formed for battle.

Captain Briant told us what was up. "Men," he said, "we have to ride hard and fast. While the rest of the regiment keeps the Rebs busy here, we can outflank them by way of a canyon to the north and come up behind their guns. In column of twos . . . by the left flank, ho!" The rain had not ceased, though it had settled down to a steady drizzle that made my uniform stick to my body like I was a half-drowned cat in a gunnysack. Cochran's hair was plastered down over the sides of his face, and he winced every time he plucked a couple of strands loose from his hurt. The horses were so soaked and muddied that except for patches, blazes, and stars, they might all have been the same color.

We slipped and slid as we circled first north, then east, then back south again. We followed an unguarded canyon that Captain Briant believed would give us the drop on Johnny Reb.

The last quarter mile was so steep and so treacherous of footing that Briant ordered us to dismount and lead our critters. I think he was afraid a horse would take a tumble and in that spot carry half his command away downstream, so caution was the word.

Before we had reached the head of the gully, we heard the boom of cannon fire. This meant we were near our objective, but it also meant that, down below, our boys were caught under the falling shells that rained on the Tullahoma road.

Captain Briant spread us out in line of battle just below the crest of the hill and had us mount up. So far no Reb picket had spotted us it seemed, and our surprise attack remained a surprise.

This time I was in the middle of the line and back about three rows from the front. "Steady," I urged Dobbs, who was showing signs of impatience. His horse, a great, tall bay, was champing at the bit and prancing sideways. "Remember the dressing-down I got from Cate, and keep your mount steady." Our carbines were still in their scabbards, it being almost impossible to manage a galloping horse and aim a rifle at the same time. Every trooper had his side arm cocked and drawn, the horses dancing nervously and sensing the excitement from every mounted man.

Then Captain Briant hollered, "Charge!" and all impatience was unleashed as we swept over the brow of the rise a hundred yards from guns.

I could see it plainly. There was a battery of four Napoleons, five-inch cannons that could throw solid shot or canister. Each gun had a crew of four men, plus there was a company of infantry to protect the battery from just such an assault as ours.

As our charge swirled down from the heights, the Confederate gun captain cooly ordered two of his weapons to pivot in place to face us. The soldiers guarding the cannon were already on one knee, firing into our ranks. Just ahead of me a man threw up his hands to grasp his face and then toppled from the saddle. His horse plunged on, riderless. I fired my Colt until I emptied all six rounds, then replaced it in the cross-draw holster and drew my saber. An instant later the pair of Reb guns blasted and a flurry of canister tore across the field.

Lead balls like giant shotgun pellets mowed through us. Twenty men in our front rank went down, but whether they were wounded or their horses shot from under, I could not say. Forty yards away the cannons unleashed another volley. Like hail on young corn, the new leading row of my comrades disintegrated in blood and shredded uniforms.

Then my rank was heading the charge. It was divine providence, and no other explanation, that there was no more time for the secesh gunners to reload. I rode down on the line of their infantry. A grizzled corporal in a floppy slouch hat drew a bead on my breastbone and pulled the trigger, but his powder must have been wet, for the gun misfired.

I swatted his bayonet aside with my saber, then brought it down backhanded across his shoulders as I spurred past him. I kneed the dun into a tight turn just as another gray-clad soldier yanked the ramrod free from his musket barrel. The left shoulder of my horse hit the Reb in the chest, making him drop his weapon and sending him spinning into a gun limber. He flipped over the wooden-spoked wheel like he was vaulting a fence, but how he landed I did not see.

A third opponent, sensing that I would be on top of him before he could reload, clubbed his rifle and swung it at my chest, intending to sweep me out of the saddle. Holding the saber point downward, to my left, I caught the blow on the guard and fended it off. Then, for want of any other stratagem, I kicked him in the chin. The lean, longhaired private was knocked to his knees, but as he fell he was already drawing a knife that was half the length of my saber.

Then I was clear on the other side of the melee and the fighting was all behind me. As I twisted the dun horse to the left, he snorted and reared. A bullet cut both reins just under his chin as cleanly as a blade would have done.

I still only had one foot in a stirrup and was without any control over the plunging buckskin. When he shied toward the trees I was instantly flat on my back in the mud. The saber was jarred loose from my grip and flipped away.

The secesh with the straggly hair loomed over me, raising his knife with a two-handed grip. He looked like a butcher with a cleaver, and I was the hog carcass to be split.

There was no time to roll out of the way and no method to deflect the blow. There was only the barest instant in which I shouted out to God to save me, and then the weapon flashed toward me.

Midway in its descent, the Reb's swing checked abruptly, and he crumpled sideways. It has always seemed to me since that day that I saw the impact of the bullet that struck him in the chest before I heard the pistol shot that launched it, even though it came from only a few yards away.

Sergeant Cate leaned over and extended his hand to

me, helping me to my none-too-steady feet. "Up you get then," he said. "You shouldn't drop your saber like that, Jesse," he scolded, "you might want for it." He kicked the heavy-bladed bowie away from the dead Rebel's hand as he holstered the revolver with which he had saved my life.

It seemed that Cate was mighty calm and easy for the midst of a battle, but the truth of it was, the fight was over. The remaining secesh fled down the slope, abandoning the cannon and their dead and wounded.

We had captured the battery, successfully protected our column on the road below, and taken a handful of prisoners as well. The Reb soldier catapulted over the gun limber by my furious charge was still cowering behind the wagon wheel. He was no more than fifteen years of age, and his face was as innocent of whiskers as a girl's.

"Come on out of there, son," I said. "You aren't hurt bad, are you?" He rose with both hands in the air, and he was trembling like an aspen leaf in a high wind. "Turn 'round and march yourself up to that sergeant yonder," I ordered. The boy stood rooted in place, as if he were wearing two hundred pounds of chains. "What ails you? Are you shot?"

Shaking violently from blond head to bare feet, the boy replied, "You gonna shoot me in the back?"

I snorted. "I don't aim to shoot you at all! What foolishness are you spouting?"

"You ain't gonna shoot me?" he asked again doubtfully.

"Not as long as you behave," I snapped, tiring of the absurd exchange. "Where'd you get such nonsense?"

"Old Bedford . . . Gen'rl Forrest . . . told us you Yanks shoot prisoners."

"Well, we don't!" Then a thought struck me. "But you say your outfit belongs to Forrest?"

The boy stretched upward with extravagant pride, in direct contradiction to his earlier alarm. "Morton's battery," he said. "Light artillery for Gen'rl Nathan Bedford Forrest!"

There was a hurried conference with Captain Briant. Cate and I were involved, while Melvin Long, Dobbs, and Cochran listened in. "Morton's battery, by heaven!" Briant exclaimed. "Then we are on to Forrest, sure as sunrise."

"Yessir," Sergeant Cate agreed. "That young Reb prisoner . . . when he found out he was not to be shot, he was so full of hisself he couldn't leave off talkin'."

Since crossing Guy's Gap and beginning the assault on the slope leading to Tullahoma, there had been no certain news about Forrest's location. And, as Captain Briant muttered to himself three or four times, keeping track of Forrest was still our main mission. "And tell me again what the boy said about Old Bedford's whereabouts."

"Said Gen'rl Forrest was coming from way over in

Columbia but he was gonna get here any time now and kick the holy stuffing out of us at Wartrace," I volunteered.

"Wartrace, eh?" Briant mused. "That's behind us already. We are overtaking the fleeing secesh so fast we'll pin Bragg's whole command against the Duck River at Shelbyville . . . and what will Forrest do about it? Will he strike us in the rear, or will he swing south and meet us head-on before the ford?"

It was not for a lowly private like me, or even a sergeant like Cate to comment on these musings, and so we waited respectfully till Briant made up his mind. "All right," he announced finally, "we must prepare for both possibilities. Sergeant Cate, I want you to ride to General Granger with the infantry division. I expect you'll find his headquarters near Wartrace. Warn him about the possible flank assault. Dodson, you come with me."

"Yesssir," I said, saluting. "Where are we going?"

"To see the colonel," he said, mounting his big chestnut horse. "If he agrees, the Third Regiment is going to ride like thunder for the crossing of the Duck River and be waiting for General Bedford Forrest to come waltzing into our arms."

It came as no surprise to me that Colonel Minnis was quick to leap to the same conclusion as Captain Briant. If our regiment could speed ahead to Shelbyville, we would cut off the Confederate line of retreat, trapping their forces between us and General Granger's foot soldiers coming along the road . . . and the biggest prize of all would be Old Bedford himself!

—————>•◊•<—————

It was afternoon when the Third Regiment came up to the outskirts of Shelbyville. A lieutenant of the First Middle Tennessee Cavalry raced up to our colonel. He was galloping full bore as if he would not stop till Nashville, but when he spotted the regimental colors, he set his gray horse back on its haunches. In the mud of the rain-soaked road, the beast skidded twenty feet before "whoa" became a reality.

"Colonel Braddock's compliments," he reported with a salute. "He asks that you come ahead on, double quick. The Reb baggage train is still on Skull Camp Bridge, but we can't get at 'em on account o' the Reb rear guard."

The order to move forward at a quick trot was relayed down to company level before the words had even finished tumbling out of our colonel's mouth. That shavetail lieutenant whipped his lathered horse around alongside and delivered the rest of his report on the move.

"We've had us a running fight since midmorning," he said. "Been trying to come at the wagons, but a troop of cavalry plus about six hundred Alabama boys is between us and the bridge. The whole Reb army is gettin' away!"

As we drew near the town of Shelbyville, we could see the truth of the matter for ourselves. The direct route through the city to the crossing of the Duck River was blocked with overturned wagons and heaps of grain bags. The other approaches were likewise guarded by grim-faced men in gray. About a quarter mile farther on, a thin streak of black smoke was creeping up into the afternoon sky.

"Lieutenant," our colonel demanded, "tell your commander to stay in line of battle, firing so as to make the Rebs keep their heads down. When he hears our bugle sound, clear your men out of the way!" The junior officer snapped another salute and spurred away.

"By gum!" Melvin Long said. "We're gonna see somethin' now!"

"Why, what's gonna happen?" a nervous Norm Dobbs hissed at me from his spot behind me in the column.

"Reb rear guard has kept our boys from lambasting their retreat," I explained, "but the bridge is still intact. If we can bust past, maybe we can head 'em off."

"But what about us?" Dobbs persisted. The damp weather stretched down his uniform so that he looked even leaner and more scarecrowlike than usual.

"Well," I said, nodding at Sergeant Cate's order for us to check our sidearms and putting fresh caps on my Colt, "let me put it to you this way: Did you ever go on a fox hunt?"

"Me?" Dobbs gulped, fumbling with his tin of

percussion caps and dropping a handful in the mud. "I never been near a fox."

"Well then, laddie-buck," remarked Cate, coming back up the column on the other side and overhearing the conversation. "All I can say is, hold on to your hat!"

Before Dobbs could ask yet another question about what he meant, it was "Forward—at the walk . . . trot . . . canter," and we were off. We stayed in a column of twos as a pair of light cannons opened up on us from behind the makeshift ramparts of meal sacks. Fortunately, they were firing high. Our advance was so swift that they could not adjust quickly enough to bring the guns to bear. We rode forward with a rattle of musketry before us and the explosions of the shells behind.

When our bugler sounded the charge we were no more than four hundred yards from the Rebs. We saw the boys of First Middle Tennessee break their skirmish line and bunch up behind wagons so as to get out of our way as we thundered forward.

The next bugle call split our column of twos apart into two streams of mounted blue, and then split it again so that four lines of galloping troopers were attacking. One column each was to the left and right, and the two in the center were aimed straight down Main Street.

There was one volley of concentrated rifle fire from the defenders, and then we were among them. Only we did not stop to mix it up in front of the town. Our aim was not to capture Shelbyville but to cut off the retreat or, failing that, to take the bridge before the Rebs burned it, protecting their retreating supply train.

I saw Captain Briant, at the head of the column on my left, direct his bay horse directly toward a barricading wagon bed. Firing his pistol to the right and the left, he jammed home his spurs and lifted the bay over the obstruction. Astonished Rebs actually held their fire as he soared over them and continued galloping down Main Street toward the river. After him two horses were shot down, but the next three riders also vaulted the barrier safely.

The eight men in front of me in file fanned out as we approached the line of meal bags. Our lead rider, Corporal Pym, was shot through the body and killed, but as his corpse tumbled over, his foot caught in the stirrup, and he was dragged alongside the frantic horse. The panicked animal turned broadside to the firing line and ran parallel to the earthworks, spoiling the aim of the Johnny Rebs.

So it was that all of us who came after jumped the Rebel line safely and clattered on toward the bridge. I scattered four shots right and left so as to make the hurdle easier for those coming after me, and in that way most of Company F passed the Confederate line uninjured.

Just because we had crossed the first obstacle did not mean our fight was over. Ahead of us, filling the town square that opened before the bridge, was a tumbling mass of men. Mounted troopers swinging sabers clashed together and wove through dismounted men waving bayonets.

There were about a hundred secesh opposing us at the bridge, about half of them cavalrymen. At first they outnumbered us, but more of our regiment successfully passed into the town, and the sound of firing coming from behind us was slackening. I shot at one feller coming at me with a pigsticker and at another who was drawing a bead on me with a shotgun, thus emptying my revolver. I felt no perforations, so I must at least have made them jump back.

Captain Briant was engaged with a stocky, dark-complected man of forty years or so. The Reb had a curly brown beard. He fought skillfully but almost negligently, as if his real attention was on what was happening around him. He kept sneaking glances up the river.

This was all I had opportunity to note before my own attention was diverted elsewhere. A brawny Reb sergeant with a coal-black beard and eyes to match spurred straight at me. He was waving a heavy, straight-edged saber about as thick as a fence post. When our blades collided, I felt the blow clear up and down my spine; made my teeth rattle.

His weapon was much heavier than mine and as difficult to ward off as a sledgehammer, but mine was the quicker on the recovery. I slashed at his face, making him throw up his arm to protect his good looks, and thereby I nicked him below the elbow. He swung back at me with his sharpened club but missed when I ducked below the arc. When my weapon flickered toward him again it pinked his sword arm, and his saber clattered to the ground.

Then the bridge exploded with a roar! The far end blew apart in a shower of splinters. There must have been jugs of coal oil on top of gunpowder, because in an instant the flames were everywhere, devouring the wooden structure.

From both sides of the fray came our other two columns of men. They had cut their way into town by other routes and now attacked the square from both east and west.

This changed the odds completely. Now we were about three hundred in blue against less than half that many graybacks. I heard Colonel Minnis call on the Rebs to throw down their arms and surrender.

To my amazement, the next sound that rang in my ears was the Reb bugler blowing charge! A column of twenty or thirty mounted graycoats, led by Old Bedford himself, hacked at full speed into our midst. The trapped Confederates, and there were about a hundred of them, massed together with the newcomers and busted through our encircling ring. Swinging sabers and clubbed pistols, the Reb troopers knocked us aside without fear of being shot. They knew that those of us who still had ammunition could not fire for fear of hitting our own men.

Skull Camp Bridge at Shelbyville was built on the

edge of a twenty-foot-high limestone bluff. Without breaking stride, every one of those cavalrymen put his mount at the leap and launched into the air above the river. I had never seen anything like it, and judging by the expressions on the faces of my comrades, neither had anyone else!

About half of the escaping troopers did not land well and were knocked from their horses, and some others were shot down while swimming across. But about thirty riders, including the bearded sergeant, who I had thought was my prisoner, emerged on the other side to clamber up the rocky slope and disappear into the trees south of the river. We made no attempt to follow.

Leading the band who made the successful flight, leaping his horse the farthest out into the stream and shouting hoarsely for the others to follow, was General Forrest. Captain Briant reined up next to me as we watched the last of the Rebs disappear from view. The tall Confederate cavalry officer stayed at the water's edge, heedless of the occasional minié ball that still spattered into the stream near him. When the last of his men had made the crossing, he, too, took his leave.

"Divided his force even in the face of our attack . . . held us off till the baggage train got across . . . destroyed the bridge so we cannot quickly follow in anything like adequate numbers . . . counterattacked and rescued his men," Briant mused to no one in particular. "That," he said pointing with his saber at the back of the Rebel general, "that, was Nathan Bedford Forrest."

A dispatch rider galloped up and handed the captain a note. He read it, grinned ruefully, and tipped his hat to the departing Rebs. "And, if that were not enough," he added, "while we were engaged here, another five thousand secesh troops crossed unopposed upstream from here."

I could scarcely credit it, but Forrest's successful escape across the Duck River was the end of the Tullahoma campaign for the Third Regiment and nearly the end for all Union pursuit. Because of our losses, which were thankfully more to mounts than to men, we were withdrawn from the front lines and placed in reserve.

When General Granger arrived in Shelbyville with our infantry, he feared a counterattack by Forrest's cavalry and so put off for a day sending the troops across the river. This delay gave the Rebs the chance they needed to reform their columns and put some distance between the two armies.

There was some skirmishing that went on as other units of the boys in blue pursued the Confederates south, but no more pitched battles and no more chances to bring Forrest to bay. So an opportunity to inflict important damage on the Rebels was lost because of fear and indecision, and, to give the devil his due, because of the cunning and courage of Bedford Forrest.

All of which is not to say that Rosy's offensive had not been successful. In nine days we had pushed Bragg and his graybacks out of Middle Tennessee and back into Alabama; kicked them out of territory they had held for a year.

Back in Camp Spear in Nashville, I got to read the first newspaper I had seen since the campaign started. I scanned the pages of the *Nashville Sentinel* for stories about our exploits. "Here it is," I said at last, as Dobbs and Cochran peered over my shoulder around the campfire. "President Lincoln sent a telegram to Rosy to congratulate him; said to tell his men they did well."

"Page sixteen!" Cochran exploded. "Might as well have left it out altogether! How come we are buried back so far?"

The answer was there in black and white: Besides what we had accomplished, General U. S. Grant had accepted the surrender of Vicksburg at last and . . . in a little town none of us had ever heard of . . . Gettysburg, Pennsylvania . . . Robert E. Lee's push to take the war onto Northern soil had by heroic efforts been thwarted.

"Is that all it says about us?" Dobbs fussed, dripping grease from his bacon and hardtack sandwich onto the newsprint.

"'Fraid so," I agreed. "Seems Gettysburg and Vicksburg are more important stories than us."

"Humph!" Cochran pouted, fingering the nearly vanished scratch on his jaw. "I come nigh getting my head blown off, and nobody takes no notice!" He took some consolation from the fact that Sergeant Cate had boasted of skinning Old Bedford, but Cochran did not wave this in the sergeant's face, of course.

As for me, though the news for the Union cause was everywhere good, it gave my spirits only the smallest of lifts. There was still no word about the fate of my son; no amount of good news from the war could make up for that. More: The Rebs had been forced out of Middle Tennessee, but they still held the east, and I could not go home.

Worst of all: The letters from my Alcie-gal—the perfumed epistles as dear to me as breath itself—stopped coming, and there was no wind from east of the Cumberlands to tell me why.

CHAPTER 5

CAMP SPEAR II
LATE SUMMER, 1863

Sunday as a day of rest had a peculiar meaning in the army. The Sabbath was the only day when no drill occurred and our duties were reduced to policing the camp and caring for the stock.

In the other hours that remained, we were allowed to recreate ourselves. Though gambling was officially forbidden, some men spent the entire day of relaxation with greasy, pasteboard rectangles playing bluff or challenging the monte bank or bucking the faro table. It seemed that some fellers had actually anticipated profiting from their enlistments and arrived at Camp Spear with all the accoutrements of gambling parlors. They had no difficulty finding lambs eager to be sheared either.

Others of us occupied our time reading, writing letters home, mending our clothing, or catching up on the laundry. There was at that time no chaplain for our regiment so Sunday services were not available in camp.

Now soldiers are no better and no worse than the run of the populace when it comes to spiritual matters. Them as were given to vice brought it with them to the army, and those of the Christian faith packed their beliefs along to enlistment too. It is true that many found their faith to be sorely challenged by their new surroundings and the temptations that come from being young and away from home.

I had just stabbed my thumb for the third time trying to darn the same sock. "Ouch," I muttered.

Melvin Long, newly made corporal, laughed at me. "You aren't cut out to be a seamstress, Jesse! Stick to mending saddles!"

I inspected the drop of blood on the pad of the injured digit and agreed. With that I tucked needle and thread back into the cloth pouch called by the soldiers a *housewife* and announced, "Melvin, I am in need of something to take my mind off home."

"Card game?" he offered.

I shook my head. "I'm no gambler," I said. "I hate losing more than I like winning, so it's no fun for me."

"I already know you're not a drinking man, Jesse," Long acknowledged. "Well, it is Sunday. Care to go to church?"

"You mean we can?"

Melvin nodded. "Sure enough. Rosy Rosecrans made it a general order that any soldier who wants leave to attend services can have it. All we got to do is see the captain."

Visions of singing and good fellowship rose up before me. "What are we waiting for? Let's see who else wants to go along."

We found Cochran and Dobbs trading haircuts. Cochran had been ordered by Sergeant Cate to do something about his straggly hair; said it might improve Cochran's shooting if he could see what he was aiming at.

Dobbs had already figured out that in an exchange with Cochran, one always made out better by receiving Cochran's contribution first. Otherwise he could be very persuasive with reasons why he could never pay you back.

In this instance, Cochran had done a credible job of trimming Dobbs's noggin. Aside from a few spikes that stuck up on his crown and the fact that his bangs marched uphill, it was not entirely without merit.

It was now time for the two to swap positions. Cochran took his position on a low round of pine wood. "Care to go to church with us?" I asked. "Melvin says we can get passes to go into Nashville for services. He's off seeing the captain about it right now."

Dobbs pulled up a three-legged stool close to Cochran's back. Tucking one long, spindly leg up to his chin, he contemplated the bushy thicket of hair as if surveying where best to attack it. He had a straight razor tucked in the pocket of his fatigue blouse. The other barbering tools lay near to hand. "Not up to me," he said. "Not 'less Cochran wants to wait on his haircut."

"I guess we'll pass, Jesse," Cochran said. "Gotta get cleaned up, or Cate will have at me with the pruning shears."

"I understand," I said.

Dobbs flourished a pair of scissors next to Cochran's ear and gave a few practice snips. "Ouch!" Cochran complained. "Cut 'em off, don't yank 'em out!"

"Sorry," Dobbs acknowledged. "Must be dulled. I'll use this other pair."

The second cutting tool applied to Dobbs had a similar result, except that while it would not cut hair, it did a fine job of nipping out a small piece of Cochran's ear.

"Great balls of fire!" Cochran spouted. "What are you playing at?"

"Sorry," Dobbs repeated. "Must both be dull. I'll just touch 'em up a mite with the whetstone."

I passed him the stone, but in his present configuration as a human pretzel, Dobbs could not get purchase enough to sharpen the edge. He unfolded his limbs to stand upright. "Won't take a second," he promised.

As Dobbs levered himself erect he somehow fumbled the whetstone and the two pairs of scissors. For an instant he looked like a juggler doing a particularly dangerous act. Then one after the other, he dropped all three implements.

The whetstone hit Cochran on the head. Both pairs of scissors fell point downward, impaling themselves in the top of the pine round, right between Cochran's legs. One of them pinned a scrap of trouser fabric to the wood.

Cochran blinked before yanking the scissors free. Standing up carefully as if afraid to make any sudden moves, he eyed the razor still in Dobbs's pocket. "You know, Jesse," he said. "Think I'll change my mind and go along with you to church. Guess I'll take my chances with Sergeant Cate after all."

There was time for us four to get curried and combed and make it to the Cumberland Baptist Church before the last verse of the opening hymn, "My Faith Looks Up to Thee." Some of the parishioners looked askance at us as we entered. Two ladies whom we passed twitched their skirts aside, but little we thought of that.

The hymn-singing continued through "Jesus, Lover of My Soul," and "Sweet Hour of Prayer," and then Pastor Bergman stood up to preach. My sweet meditations of home and family and our little country church vanished in an instant, but for the sake of courtesy, we four remained for the entire hour that he spoke.

Pastor Bergman took for his text the deliverance of the Israelites from the grasp of Midian. "All the citizens of the sovereign state of Tennessee have an obligation to resist tyranny," he said. "Should we live like the unanointed Gideon, thrashing our wheat in secret so our oppressors do not steal from us? Shall we be forced to bow down in idol worship of the bearded pagan deity who sits on his throne in Washington?"

Murmurs of "No, no, never," echoed around the hall, and we four received numerous piercing looks.

"The godless invaders," Bergman continued, "who would deny us our rights and despoil us of our property must be put down! They must and shall be expelled from our midst."

When he had finished at last, the congregation sang "There Is a Fountain Filled with Blood," but we left during the benediction.

"Well, Jesse," said Long. "I don't think we'll be going back to their services."

"Naw," agreed Cochran. "There weren't none of them folks gonna invite us home to supper anyhow."

I returned to camp much sobered and worried about the outcome of the war. If the division of the country ran so deep, how could any side ever really win? Regardless of the result of battles, what could mend such a grievous breach? For how long even after the fighting stopped would the consequences of the rupture remain?

━━━▷◆◁━━━

Despite our hard knocks and long hours in the saddle on the Tullahoma campaign, our regiment lost but fifty men killed, wounded, or captured. We felt real pert and proud of ourselves. Said Cochran, "They shoulda turned us loose. I woulda chased Old Bedford clean to the Gulf! I woulda kicked Braxton Bragg's behind clean to Mexico! I woulda . . ."

At this point Sergeant Cate interrupted by poking his head in the tent flap. "Fall in for fatigue duty," he ordered. "Turn to and police the camp. Cochran, me boyo, since you are in such fine fettle, you are elected for a special privilege: Draw a pick and fall in for road building detail."

Cochran's groan and the smirks of the others at this statement were easily understood. When Camp Spear first received troops it was no more than a bare field of dirt and brush. Different commanders determined to improve the surroundings according to their personal tastes. In the case of Colonel Minnis, it was resurfacing with cobble-stones the dusty road that was the camp's main thoroughfare. Every day men were selected to haul, spread, shovel, and level chunks of limestone. In mid-July, the combination of sweltering heat and rock dust made road building a matter for regimental punishment details. Unfortunately for Cochran, there just were not enough men undergoing discipline to fill the labor company.

As the bugle sounded fatigue call, we formed ranks for the afternoon roll before being assigned the rest of the cleanup chores. It was at this lineup that Company F's replacements were introduced.

The single addition to our mess was a German recruit by the name of Blankenbeckler, Johannes Blankenbeckler. He was swart, bullnecked, and as solidly cheerful of disposition as he was fractured of English. He was instantly rechristened "Blanket," Cochran objecting that the German's other handle was too cumbersome. Blankenbeckler grinned and agreed by saying, "Ja. Blanket iss goot. Easy to remember."

"Well, say then, friend Blanket," Cochran said, oozing good fellowship and camaraderie. "How'd you like to trade duty with me today? My lumbago is acting up again, and I sure need the relief."

"Don't do it," Melvin Long warned the German. "Cochran is a beat. If he knows you are a soft touch he'll be after you all the time, and he'll never pay you back neither."

Cochran's face was contorted between flashing his ingratiating smile at Blanket and giving Long looks sharper than any bayonet. The stitches on Long's chevrons had hardly clinched tight, but even so they already limited Cochran's response to the corporal's advice. "Come on, Blanket," Cochran pleaded. "What do you say?"

"I do not know what is this soft touch, but I am new here and want to get along with my new friends. I say Ja, I will trade if the sergeant agrees."

When informed by Corporal Long of the proposed switch, Sergeant Cate surprised me. I thought he would insist that Blanket not be taken advantage of on his first day, but instead he agreed to the swap. In fact, he seemed rather pleased with the notion. "Sure and a fine idea it is too. Very well, Private Blanket, join the road crew by the flagpole. Cochran, come with me."

"Wait just a minute!" Cochran protested. "I smell a rat!"

"I have just been notified," explained Cate, waving a slip of paper under Cochran's nose, "of the need for an additional fatigue party, and I bethought to send the new man. But as matters stand, it falls to you, Private Cochran."

"But what is it?"

Cate looked as innocent as new-fallen snow. "Did I not say? It's a funeral party."

If Cochran's moaning protest had been heard in Ohio before, his lament over this new situation likely roused sleepers in Canada.

The funeral to be conducted was of a horse, not a soldier. In the fight at the Skull Camp Bridge, more animals had been wounded than people, and of these, some had come away with festering sores. It took a week to carry them off. Cochran would be joining others in digging holes wide and deep enough to inter fallen equine heroes. The corpses were dragged to the burial field by mule power, but once there, the graves had to be dug right next to each body so that the corpses could be easily tumbled in. Since this project was not done every day, and given the ninety-five degree heat, one can only imagine the horror that Cate's announcement produced in Cochran. But there was no way out. All of us had witnessed that he was the one who had suggested the swap.

As saddler, I was excused most fatigue duty so as to get caught up with the necessary repairs to bridles and saddles. About five in the afternoon, my own business required me to visit the stores and draw some more leather and saddle soap. I deliberately adjusted my route so as to pass the funeral detail, taking care to stay upwind, of course.

Long quizzed me on my return. "Did you see Cochran? How was he getting on?"

"He was loving every minute of it," I reported.

"Having a grand old time and shouting with excitement."

Corporal Long grabbed me by the arm. "Don't kid an old soldier, Jesse," he demanded. "What are you talking about?"

"It's the gospel truth," I maintained. "He was shouting 'Hurrah! Hurrah!'" Even my best poker face was not up to the occasion. "Well," I finally relented, laughing. "Maybe he was leaving the 'H' off his cheer. Truth be told, I think Private Cochran is trying to throw up his immortal soul!"

<hr/>

It was some time after Cochran had attempted to take advantage of Blankenbeckler and been outfoxed himself that Company F received one more additional recruit. This was John Quincy Hamilton III, age nineteen, who wasted no time in informing us that he was lately of Harvard University. He had only returned to his native Nashville to lend his dashing expertise to routing the Rebs. He was offended that there was no room in our tent for his two trunks of belongings and made several unkind remarks about the smell inside our home. Not that he was wrong, of course, but it seemed ungracious and lacking in tact for a newcomer to mention it.

I do not know what infraction Company F was guilty of so as to cause the colonel to favor us with Private Hamilton, but he was instantly a trial to all. If

Cochran was a deadbeat and Dobbs a bad luck Jonah, at least they were recognizable types; accepted and tolerated as such.

Hamilton was something else again. He was slender, vain, superior of attitude, and given to looking down his long, thin nose at all aspects of army life. Had he taken part in the grousing about the duty and the food, he might have had a chance for acceptance. But when every one in our mess felt that he was sneering at them as well . . .

So it became a kind of company pastime to give Hamilton plenty to be upset about.

On the very first day in camp, after drawing a uniform, it was every recruit's privilege to grouse about how ill-fitting it was, how scratchy the tight collar was, how hot the wool jacket was, and so on. This response was expected and deemed commendable.

Not so from Private Hamilton. He brought a bespoke set of three uniforms—dress, undress, and fatigue—with him to the post. He held the government-issue tunic at arm's length as if it had lately been taken from a leper. Even worse, Hamilton set about criticizing the cut of everyone else's uniform: How sloppy we all looked, how unsoldierly. He concluded by saying that he would have his manservant take orders from each of us to supply made-to-order livery by week's end. From the mirror gleam of his cavalier boots to the downturned, catfish-like set to his mouth, John Quincy Hamilton III was hated by one and all.

It was more than Cochran could bear, and this time he had Corporal Long's connivance in his scheming. Said Cochran to Hamilton, "You sure are right! Just look at Dodson there: grease marks on his trouser legs, tarnished cap badge . . . Jesse, you are a disgrace to the outfit. A disgrace! Ain't that so, Corporal?"

"Certainly is! Dodson, I'll bet you have even forgotten to put the shoeblacking on your umbrella."

I hung my head in shame and remorse. "It's true, Corporal," I admitted. "Even worse, I don't know where I have mislaid it."

Hamilton's ears twitched. "Umbrella?" he demanded. "No one informed me. I was not issued an umbrella. Why was I not issued one?"

Corporal Long looked shocked. "That dash-dash-dashed quartermaster sergeant," he exclaimed. "How dare he shortchange you that a'way; and you a young gentleman of quality as you are. That is not to be tolerated! You march right back to that sharper and demand that he furnish you with your umbrella at once!"

Being slighted did not square with Hamilton's opinion of himself. Moreover, correcting the failings of someone he thought of as a clerk was securely in his brief as a rising member of society. Hamilton set out immediately to amend the wrong he had suffered. The rest of our mess trooped along to watch the fun.

Now the quartermaster sergeant bore more than a passing physical resemblance to a red-bearded grizzly bear. Moreover, his usual demeanor was like to a bear also, only not as friendly.

Hamilton's life was in jeopardy, though he did not recognize his danger. Crossing Sergeant Jasper was always chancy, but was particularly so when Hamilton called, pushing through a crowd of men to the head of the line and demanding Jasper's attention. Sergeant Jasper had only just been informed that instead of going off duty, he must attend to the mustering-in needs of two new and unexpected companies of troops. Also, Sergeant Jasper had partaken too freely of medicinal spirits on the previous evening, and he was experiencing a disturbance inside his head like all the church bells of Nashville ringing at once.

"Sergeant," Hamilton said, politely enough.

"Get back in line," Jasper growled without looking up.

"Sergeant," Hamilton tried again, louder. "This will just take a moment."

To Jasper's credit, he tried to ignore Hamilton, showing his irritation only in the force with which he slammed a pile of clothing down on the counter and snarled, "Next!"

Then Hamilton made a fatal misjudgment. He snapped his fingers at Jasper, as no doubt he was in the habit of doing with inattentive waiters. "Sergeant!" he said, imperiously. (*Snap! Snap!*) "You have made a mistake that must be corrected at once."

I do not know which aspect of this speech most

infuriated Jasper: the imputation of an error or the demand by a lowly recruit that something be done immediately. Peering around the doorframe or peeping in the window, Cochran, Long, Dobbs, and I saw Jasper momentarily stunned into silence. It was like slapping a bull on the nose; the very temerity of it surprised the quartermaster sergeant, but as Cochran once remarked, the only safe way to slap Sergeant Jasper was with a sledgehammer.

In any case, here is what happened: Jasper gave a bellow that would have done credit to either bull or bear. Then, slamming his fist down on the counter, he broke the wooden planks in two, spilling a hundred pairs of trousers on the floor. The foremost recruits in the line trampled on those behind getting back outside. Hamilton was left confronting Jasper from three feet away. I tend to think that John Quincy Hamilton III may have had some reservations about going ahead with his complaint. Indeed, the rest of us wondered if we had gone too far.

"Now!" roared Jasper. "You have my full attention. What did you say you wanted?"

Hamilton cleared his throat with an audible quaver, but we grudgingly conceded that he did not shrink back as much as we expected. To Dobbs I whispered, "I'd be heading back toward Harvard by now."

"Me too," Dobbs agreed. "When I see a runaway locomotive coming toward me, I always skedaddle!"

"I did not receive my government-issue umbrella, and I want it."

"Your what?!"

"Umbrella. You failed to supply me with an umbrella."

It was truly amazing to see how fast a three-hundred-pound man like Quartermaster Sergeant Jasper could move. Before any of us could blink, Jasper leaped for Hamilton's throat. Only the fact that the sergeant's feet tangled in the heap of trouser legs saved Hamilton from destruction.

Red beard flying over his shoulder like a regimental battle flag, Jasper landed with the force of a brick chimney blown over in a high wind. He most certainly would have crushed the life out of Hamilton had he connected.

But Hamilton's determination had dissolved just in time. As Jasper came crashing down, John Quincy Hamilton III squirted out the door of the supply depot and ran for it.

"Most likely a track and field star at Harvard," Melvin Long remarked.

"Think he'll be back for his umbrella?" Dobbs wanted to know.

Cochran shook his head. "If I was him," he said, "and I thought I would ever have to face Sergeant Jasper again . . ."

"Yeah?"

"I'd sooner go naked for all three years of my enlistment."

"Jesse, pour me a skosh of coffee, will you?" Melvin Long suggested at supper one evening.

"You dunderheaded ninny, Dobbs!" Sergeant Cate shouted the next day on the target range. "Put your thumb down when you squeeze that trigger! You came within a skosh of putting your own eye out!"

"Hurry up, will you, Cochran?" I demanded on fatigue. "If you don't move a skosh faster shifting that tack we won't get finished before reveille tomorrow!"

It seemed that when the boredom of camp life became too great, one of the unacknowledged pastimes was making up and using newfangled words. *Skosh* became a jack-of-all-words meaning "a little, a small amount of anything." No one ever claimed to have made it up or even to have heard it somewheres else; it just made its appearance in camp and within two days was in common use.

After our rebuff at the local church, the search for a meaningful way to fill our Sundays continued. To card-playing and the homely occupations of time off-duty was added dime novels. "Hey, Cochran," Dobbs demanded, "ain't you finished with the *Gold Fiend* yet?"

"Just a skosh," Cochran replied. "Here, look at this new one I got over to the sutler's."

"What is it?"

"A real gimcrack! See: *East and West, A Daring Adventure by Land and Sea*."

"All right," Dobbs acknowledged. "Give it here."

Into this stifled atmosphere strode Private Hamilton.

Only a week had passed since the quartermaster sergeant had rubbed some of the shine off Hamilton's upturned nose. In that time the college student had sulked and, by refusing to laugh at himself, had put even more distance between himself and the rest of us.

His arrival on Sunday afternoon was different. He had a spring in his step, and he looked around eagerly. Behind him was another young man, this one in the uniform of a parson.

Hamilton focused on our little group and came directly toward us. "Ah," he said cheerfully. "Dobbs, Cochran, Blanket, I want you to meet a dear and distinguished friend of mine . . . the Reverend Morris Larson."

We all stood and dusted ourselves off, shuffling in an embarrassed fashion because of our relaxed dress. Cochran thrust the two yellow-jacketed novels into Blanket's hands behind his back, and Long nudged a pack of cards under the tent flap with the toe of his boot. We mumbled greetings.

Hamilton continued, "Morris, I mean Reverend Larson, is an old college chum of mine. We met most providentially, and he agreed to accompany me back to camp." Hamilton paused here to let a gaze of deep concern linger on the face of each of us. "I want you all to know that I recognize how bad a start I got off to, but I wish to make amends. Realizing how hungry you are for spiritual nourishment, I have prevailed upon Reverend Larson to preach to us today."

"Truly?" I said at this unexpected development.

"This is real kind, Reverend. You may have heard that we were not exactly made to feel welcome in the Nashville churches."

"Shocking!" Larson announced with a look of righteous indignation. "To deny you spiritual consolation in your hour of need."

"There's just one thing," Hamilton said smoothly. "I have not yet approached Captain Briant to ask his permission to assemble the men, and in fact I don't feel that I am the one to do so. But if a deputation such as you five would go, I am certain he could have no objection."

I confess that I had some misgivings at this point, but Cochran and the others were so instantly enthusiastic that I felt guilty for my lack of eagerness to join in.

In any case, within fifteen minutes we had petitioned the captain for permission to muster the men for a sermon. Larson promised that it would be rousing, stirring, and uplifting. True to our promise to Hamilton, he was not present at the officer's tent, nor was he credited with having sponsored the notion.

"Fall in for sermon," was the unusual command that followed the bugle calling assembly.

We lined up in ranks facing the flagpole while the Reverend Larson mounted a wagon bed from which to address us. "Men," Captain Briant began, "I know you will be pleased to give your attention to this man of God who has graciously come to share his spiritual insights with us. And I know you will also want to express your gratitude to those of your comrades who arranged this event: Long, Dobbs, Cochran, Blankenbeckler, and Dodson. And now, Reverend Larson."

Larson stepped forward, and then oddly seemed overcome with the gaze of the crowd. He appeared speechless, even thunderstruck. "What's the matter, Parson?" called out some unknown in the crowd. "Can't you preach?"

"Can't I preach!" Larson roared. "I know this book from lid to lid! From Generation to Revolution! For the whangdoodle mourneth for her firstborn and fleeth to Mount Hepsidam!"

That was all the farther he got, for an outraged Captain Briant started toward the impostor only one step in advance of us. The fictitious parson had his escape well planned, however, and sprinted ahead of our vengeance to exit on horseback from the camp.

The damage was already done, of course. The five of us were each given three days' punishment for improper conduct: We were made to stand atop cracker boxes on one leg. Of course the soldiers' code forbade us from laying off the blame on Hamilton.

Worse even than the punishment were the reactions of the rest of our company. The other Christians were embarrassed and chagrined at the mockery, while the routinely profane found the whole thing a great lark and promptly applauded Hamilton . . . not at all the kind of witness we would have wanted.

Only the stoical Blankenbeckler seemed unfazed. He looked up from a thin red volume he was reading and observed, "In this world you will troubles have. Sometimes a skosh more, sometimes a skosh less."

CHAPTER 6

*Mc*CMINN
COUNTY
SEPTEMBER 1863

For six weeks, from July to mid-August 1863, our regiment drilled, rode guard along train tracks from Nashville to Murfreesboro, drilled, went on scouting expeditions toward Sparta, drilled, chased a false report that Old Bedford was moving toward Kentucky, and drilled. And in our spare time we . . .

Meanwhile, the war seemed at a stalemate. Bobby Lee had been tossed out of Pennsylvania, but was then allowed to escape unmolested back to Virginia. Cochran said that the goggle-eyed General Meade, who had stopped the Rebs at Gettysburg, had gone and caught "Federal commander disease": the slows. Somehow it seemed that no Union general was ever able to put two victories together back-to-back.

By August fifteenth Camp Spear was so completely surfaced with cobblestones that its streets were in better repair than those of Nashville proper. 'Course, truth be told, some of those selfsame cobblestones had once graced Nashville's streets before being midnight requisitioned.

When we finally got a true report of General Forrest's whereabouts, it like to broke my heart: He made his new headquarters at Kingston, east of the Cumberlands and thirty miles *north* of my home near Athens. Much was made of how the Rebs were now on the defensive and how Rosy was getting ready to hit them again somewhere. But all the idle speculation chafed me. I still had no word of the location of my son and no news from home.

Then, just when the inactivity of camp life and the anxiety over my family were about to make me despair, something happened. Colonel Minnis sent for Captain Briant to ride over to regimental headquarters to confer. In about an hour Briant was back, and though it was nearly supper he ordered the bugler to sound assembly. Here is what we heard:

"Men," he said, "General Rosecrans is ready to move again. This time we are going to boot the secesh out of Chattanooga and maybe out of Tennessee altogether."

There was a rousing cheer at this. In one instant, all the terrors of the Tullahoma campaign and all the tedium of Camp Spear were forgotten. Victory and glory were once more the order of the day. When the shouting died, Briant continued, "The Third Regiment is to remain in Nashville, guarding the supply lines from here southward."

An audible groan swept over the ranks. What had been excitement changed again to gloom. In fact, the despondency was even deeper when it sank in that the rest of the army would be on the move, but not us. That was the moment at which Corporal Long nudged me and nodded toward Briant's face. The captain was wearing a sly smile rather than a scowl or frown. "He knows something he's not telling," Long avowed.

"However," Briant acknowledged at last, "the guard duty will not include Company F. The colonel has asked and I have agreed that we should be temporarily assigned to General Crittenden's corps as scouts. Every man is to draw three days' rations. We leave tomorrow at dawn."

If the earlier cheers were enthusiastic, the later news produced an outburst that was deafening. Hats and haversacks were tossed in the air. Cochran, not content with pitching his own hat in the air, seized Blanket's and threw it skyward as well.

When the assembly was dismissed, Captain Briant sought me out and drew me aside for a word. "Jesse," he said, "what I am about to say will not become public knowledge for some days yet, so keep it to yourself. But since it concerns you personally, I wanted you to hear it at once."

Worries buzzed around my head like the cloud of horseflies around the stable. Chief among them was that I was to be left behind. "I know the other outfits need help with their tack," I protested, "but Franks over in

Company D has the makings of a fine saddler. Can't you get him?"

Briant laughed and shook his head. "Not that," he said. "Just the opposite, in fact. General Rosecrans wants to keep the Confederates guessing as to which direction the attack on Chattanooga will come from. Part of Crittenden's force, including our troop, is to cross the Cumberland toward the Hiwassee River. And that means . . ."

"Athens! My home . . . my farm?"

"The same," Briant agreed. "If all goes well, you'll see your place again in no more than two weeks."

⋙◆⋘

Setting out in company with a troop known as Minty's Horse, we were the advance guard of General Crittenden's Twenty-first Army Corps. We first contacted the enemy that same day; a party of opposing cavalrymen who were raiding near Sparta.

There followed three days of running fights, first along Wild Cat Creek and, later, up into the reaches of Calfkiller Creek. We were pushing the Rebs back east over the mountains, but at considerable loss to ourselves.

The skirmishes fell into a pattern: The Rebs would show themselves, fire a couple of volleys, and then fall back. When we pursued, dismounted sharpshooters would blaze away at us from ambush until we stopped to surround and eliminate each one. Every time we halted on account of one Reb, the main body would draw off in perfect safety and set up to do the whole thing over again.

On the eighteenth of August, Company F was proceeding cautiously up a draw to the southeast of Calfkiller Creek when we again came under sniper fire. The stream wound out of a brush-choked canyon between two hillsides strewed with boulders and dotted with oak and hickory trees.

We were riding in a skirmish line across about a quarter mile of hillside in advance of the main body of the troop. We had seen Rebs about a half hour earlier, and some of them had gone up this draw. Long and I were near the center of our line. "Look sharp," Long cautioned everyone. "There is plenty of cover hereabouts for bushwhackers."

We had not ridden more than another fifty feet before the crack of a rifle split the morning and Long was knocked backward out of his saddle. His horse bolted and fled.

"Dismount! Dismount!" Sergeant Cate yelled. "Use your mounts as cover."

I looped the reins of the bay I was riding over a fallen limb and knelt beside Long. "Ah, Jesse," my friend sputtered through clenched teeth. "It hurts like blazes."

"Where are you hit, Melvin?"

"My arm . . . look for me, will you, Jesse? I think he shot it clean off."

Long's left arm hung limp and blood pumped from a ragged hole in his sleeve. I whipped off the strap from his carbine and used it to make a tourniquet around his upper arm. Then I dragged him behind a rock. As I did so, another lead slug whipped past and plowed a furrow in the leaf mold near my boot. "Just take it easy, Melvin," I urged him, trying to sound calm. "I'll be back for you in a minute." When he did not respond, I saw that he had fainted.

"Sergeant," I yelled. "Long is hit bad . . . needs help."

The sound of my voice drew a third round from the sniper, clipping rock splinters just above my head.

Cate yelled, "Anybody see where those shots are coming from?"

Nobody replied.

Minutes passed without another cartridge being fired. "Dobbs," Cate ordered, "when I yell, you, me, and Hamilton are going to move up to that next clump of trees. Keep low and keep your horse between you and the hill. The rest of you, cover us."

I eased around the corner of the boulder and rested my Sharps in a crevice. Swinging the muzzle back and forth like the nose of a questing hunting dog, I attempted to aid my friends. But how could I when I had no idea where the sniper was located?

Cate shouted, and the three men burst from concealment to advance farther up the canyon. They had not covered more than a dozen feet before the Reb rifle boomed again and Dobbs's horse screamed, reared, and plunged over backward. We all sprayed the slope with return fire, but blindly and without noticeable effect. Dobbs scurried behind an oak, and the other two likewise went to the ground.

"Where is he?" Cate demanded again. "Anybody see that time?"

There was still no response.

Cate swore. "We're gonna get picked off one at a time this way!"

I studied the hillside. Trees, rocks, and brush all provided some cover, but there was only one likely spot I could see. Halfway up the incline was the stump of a hickory tree, as big around as a dining table and about table height. If it was hollow as well, the Reb sniper might be inside it. I watched carefully, but saw no movement.

"Blanket!" Cate yelled. "Move up!"

Private Blanket obeyed the command, but he was sensible about it. He drew his revolver and fired across his horse's back as he ran. When he had discharged all six rounds he jerked the horse down in a shallow depression in the earth and lay behind it. His sprint attracted another bullet that would have parted his hair had he not flopped down at exactly the moment he did.

I had seen what I expected, but in the barest blink of an eye. At the instant of Blanket's rush, a brown-haired figure, dressed in gray, rose up from inside the hickory stump, drew a bead, and fired. Then the sniper ducked down again, out of sight and protected.

He was only visible for a split second, and his perch gave him command of all the approaches to his nest. Every time he fired, he knew a charge was coming, and he stood erect and shot.

I lined up the blade sight of my carbine on the stump and reminded myself to adjust for the elevation. Firing uphill makes most shots go high. I could not afford to miss, because once he knew his hideaway was discovered, the Reb would sneak out to another, and the deadly game of hide-and-seek would continue. I could not even call out to my comrades for fear the sniper would hear and move.

So, I waited.

"Dodson," Cate ordered, "move up."

What to do now? I could see from the positions of my friends that I was the only one with a clear line of fire. Snatching my cap from my head, I reached out for a nearby stick. I mounted the hat on the dead limb, this without moving the Sharps or taking my eye from the sight. Then I bellowed, "Now!" at the top of my lungs and thrust the cap aloft. A second later my headgear went spinning away toward the creek and the Sharps bucked in my hands.

I studied the hickory stump for a long, long time. Then I stood carefully upright. "Did you get him, Jesse?" Dobbs called.

Shrugging, I turned away to see to Melvin Long. "Did you get him?" Dobbs repeated.

"He never come up no more," I said simply. "Go get the sergeant, will you? Melvin is in need of help."

⟫◆⟪

Melvin Long was lucky; as lucky as anybody can be who has just been shot. Minié balls, being soft lead and about the size of the end of my thumb, had a terrible effect on bones they hit. Limbs were usually so shattered that taking them off was the only hope of saving a feller's life.

Long's arm wound was clean through the meat, without touching the bone. Once we got the bleeding stopped, he was patched up and sent back to Nashville. In the meantime, I was made acting corporal of the outfit. Others were not so lucky; full thirty troopers of other units were killed dead or died soon after being bushwhacked on the Calfkiller or in the fight outside Bon Air.

Despite the losses inflicted on us and the other troopers of Minty's Horse, we pushed the Reb cavalry back over the Cumberlands and stood on the summit ourselves. Captain Briant took special care to explain to us what was afoot. "General Rosecrans has two corps to attack Chattanooga from the south, but he doesn't want Bragg to know it just yet. Us and the rest of Crittenden's corps are to make a big show of crossing the mountains north of Chattanooga and make the Rebs think this is the direction of the attack."

"And then what happens?" Sergeant Cate drawled.

Briant paused and reflected. He rubbed a grimy hand over his high forehead and picked an oak twig out of his burnsides. "Either Bragg will send his boys out to fight us and Rosy pounces on Chattanooga, or Bragg gets scared and calls his troops in from East Tennessee to help defend the city. If he calls them back, then we retake East Tennessee from the secesh, and then both our columns squeeze Chattanooga like a nutcracker."

We knew from captured snipers that we had been fighting members of Dibrell's Horse, a local unit of secesh Middle Tennessee boys. But east of the mountains were regular Confederate troops.

"Who are we squaring off with tomorrow?" I asked.

"Can't say for certain," Briant admitted. "But we heard tell Forrest was headquartered in Kingston."

Forrest again! Kingston was the first town of any size we would encounter once we descended the slope.

Five days later, after a careful passage of the mountains but no more fighting, we discovered that Rosy's strategy had worked. Bragg had called his forces back toward Chattanooga as far as Loudon on the Knoxville and Chattanooga railroad. We road into Kingston unopposed, except for a few small boys who spit on our shadows as we passed.

And there were not many of those incidents either. If Nashville regarded Yankee troops as invaders and

Tennesseans who wore the blue as turncoats, often the situation was reversed here. We were looked upon as liberators, only quietly, or even slyly.

Private Cochran and I were scouting ahead of the main body along the west bank of the Tennessee River. We found a small crossroads settlement, searched it for Rebs, then turned back to report.

"'Scuse me, Granny," Cochran said to an elderly woman smoking a corncob pipe under an elm tree. "Can we water our horses from your well?"

Loudly she hollered, "You blue-bellied snakes think you can come in here and take all our possessions and make free with our belongings! You just ride on outta here and go off and get yourselves shot!"

"Granny," Cochran said, baffled at the vehement outburst, "we don't want to take nothing, we just want to water our horses a skosh is all."

Underneath her breath the silver-haired woman muttered, "Swear at me."

"What?"

"Go on, do it," she hissed. "Cuss me and tell me you'll take whatever you dang well please."

I tumbled to the scheme at once. "Get away with you, you old crone!" I berated her harshly. "You skinny scarecrow of a no-good Rebel. We are going to water our horses and take whatever we've a mind to. Get back in the house, and if you're lucky, you won't get hurt."

Slipping her a wink, I reined my horse toward the pump at the side of the house. Granny returned the quick flutter of eyelashes and said softly, "God bless you boys! Be safe."

"What was all that about?" Cochran demanded when we were out of sight of the main road. "Is she tetched?"

I nodded and grinned. "Like a fox," I said. "The Rebs have held this part of the state for two years. Granny knows that to curry favor some of her neighbors would run and tell Old Bedford about how she willingly aided Yankee troopers."

"Woof!" Cochran acknowledged. "She's a sly old bird!" Then an unpleasant notion struck him. "Wait a minute! That means she thinks Old Bedford may not be really gone . . . that maybe we didn't kick him out for good!"

I dropped my chin and gave Cochran my best schoolmaster look. "I swan, Cochran," I said. "You get a star on your composition this day, yes indeed."

———◆◆◆———

General Crittenden's corps was putting on a great show, marching and countermarching and generally acting like there was three times more of them than there really was. When we went into camp for the night, every mess of eight men built three campfires, so as to convince any onlookers of the mighty host that was coming upon Chattanooga from the north. 'Course since it was so warm still, we ended up sleeping way far back from those fires. Men actually volunteered to go on picket duty so as to get out of camp and cool off.

South of Kingston, the Tennessee River was the dividing line between our forces and the Rebels. We kept to the west bank, the secesh to the east. Now that we were across the mountains, the cavalry's job as the eyes of the army was more important than ever. Even though the Twenty-first Corps was the feint and not the real assault, it still made up one-third of Rosecrans's army of the Cumberland. It would not do to get pounced on unawares.

Wherever we could ford the river, and in late summer there were plenty of places, we struck across into Rebel territory. We scouted toward Loudon and Philadelphia and finally, on the twenty-eighth of August, toward Athens. Once across the river we would range as much as twenty miles inside enemy territory.

Captain Briant cautioned us. "Men," he said, "I can't tell you the reason just yet, but we have got something real important to do. We don't know where Old Bedford is right now. He may still be up Loudon way, or he may have already pulled back toward Charleston. We need information about troop movements and intentions. Corporal Dodson?"

"Yes, sir," I responded.

"This is your home ground, is it not?"

I nodded.

"If there are any little-used paths or deserted cabins that you know about, I'd like you to point them out on the maps to Sergeant Cate and me. We may need a bolt-hole before we get back. What do you say?"

"Captain," I said, "I can go you one better than that. I been thinking about it for a day now. If you'll detail me a couple of men to ride with me as far as Tellico Junction, I'll get you all the news you need."

When I had explained myself to the captain, he drew me aside and tried to dissuade me. "If you are captured in civilian clothes you can be shot or hanged as a spy," he said. "No one is asking you to do this. Why not guide the whole troop where we can make a fight of it if we have to?"

"Captain," I said, "we'd still be outnumbered, and it's a long way back to the river. 'Sides, I know folks who will talk, if they aren't scared of being seen talking to Yankees." I did not think it the right time to tell Captain Briant of the price on my head as a Confederate deserter. It might have put him off of my idea, and I was as anxious for news of home as I was concerned about Old Bedford.

"All right," Briant agreed. "Do you want volunteers, or have you got some men in mind?"

Blanket, Cochran, and Dobbs all stepped forward. "These are the ones I was going to ask for," I said. To my surprise, Hamilton stepped forward as well.

"Very well," Briant concluded. "Leave as soon as you're ready and be back here by tomorrow night."

About a mile above Tellico Junction there was an abandoned gristmill on the bank of Walden's Creek. I did not think anyone would have put the mill back into operation in those troubled times, and we could use the place to lay up by day. That's where our squad made for, arriving just past midnight.

"No lights," Dobbs hissed after reconnoitering up ahead. "I listened for a time, and I didn't hear nothing either."

An owl hooted from the branches of a sweet gum, but no other sound could be heard except the trickle of water over stones. "Tie up the horses below the lip of the creek bank, just behind the mill," I said. "That way they'll be out of sight but handy to the back door."

We settled on the floor inside the mill and watched the stars pinwheel in the sky through the space of missing shingles. We durst not make a fire and so drank cold coffee out of our canteens and made cold supper of hardtack and cheese.

"Why do you not go on over to the postmaster's place now?" Blanket asked. "Why for daylight wait?"

"Ferguson may have folks staying over with him," I explained. "It'll look more natural if I come in when the sun is up than if I sneak in this time of night. You fellers just wait on me here," I said quietly.

"How long should we wait?" Cochran asked.

"If I'm not back one hour after sundown," I instructed, "you three hightail it back to camp."

"What'll we tell the captain?" Dobbs asked.

Shrugging, I replied, "Tell him I failed."

Early in the morning, before the rays of the sun had outlined the highest leaves of the sweet gum, I swapped my uniform for a pair of overalls and a flannel shirt. I knotted a blue-and-white-checked kerchief around my throat and pulled a tattered straw hat well down on my head. The addition of a pair of down-at-the-heels, out-at-the-toes work boots completed my transformation.

Only Blanket was awake, on watch. The other two were tucked behind the millstones, Dobbs hugging the base of the grain hopper. "You want I should wake them?" Blanket asked.

"Naw, let 'em sleep. Just keep alert for trouble," I said. "Now that the owl has gone to bed, give an ear to that 'baccy bird across the hollow. If he stops singing sudden like, it'll either be me coming back or somebody you don't want to meet."

"What iss a 'baccy bird?"

"Just listen a skosh," I instructed. "Hear that? Tobacco bird . . . 'baccy bird, we calls 'em. He says, 'Merrily we chew . . . merrily we chew.'"

East Tennessee humor was lost on Blanket.

"Never mind then. Just watch sharp if he stops sayin' that!"

I could be disguised, but there was no hiding a U.S. cavalry horse. I had no time to requisition a mule or some other homely local critter, so I walked the two miles on to Tellico Junction.

There was no light showing at the front of Ferguson's place, but a thin trickle of smoke from the chimney at the back told me R. J. was up and getting his breakfast. I circled to the kitchen door and called in my most backwoods tone, "Yo, Mistuh Ferguson. Is you at home?"

There was silence from within till I repeated my call, and then an elaborate throat-clearing vibrated the tools hanging on the wall beside the door. A rumbling cough mixed with a forceful snort put one in mind of a drowning bullfrog, if such a thing can be imagined. It was R. J., and no mistake. "Who's that callin' out yonder?" he inquired.

"Jus' me, Mistuh Ferguson . . . Ahab Trafalger."

"Ahab Traf . . . !" R. J. sputtered. Then to my great relief, he said nothing to give the game away. The screen door creaked open, and a spindly arm extended through the crack. "Well, Ahab," R. J. said. "Come on in. Haven't seen you in a coon's age. Set a spell and have some coffee."

I stepped into R. J.'s kitchen and asked nonchalantly, "Anybody else about? John Dixon, mayhap, or Jesse Dodson?"

"No one 'cept the cavalry officer sleepin' upstairs," R. J. said with a significant raise of his bushy eyebrows. "He's passin' through McMinn County, looking for deserters. His men is out in my barn right now."

So my instincts and a gracious providence had kept me from a disaster! What would my story have been had I waltzed into Tellico in the middle of the night?

R. J. leaned his head close to my ear and hissed.

"What are you doin' here, Jesse? The woods from Niota to Noneberg is crawling with Rebs!" Then in a louder tone he remarked, "You still runnin' 'shine up the Hiwassee?"

"And how!" I agreed forcefully. "Them army fellers is a right thirsty bunch." Then I murmured, "I've had no letters for months! How's Alcie and my babies?"

"It's bad, Jesse," R. J. whispered back. "Reb cavalry has run off all your stock and cleaned out your larder. Alcie is just scrapin' by." He almost blew my eardrum out when without warning he shouted, "You'll be wantin' sour mash then, Ahab?"

"Can I see her?" I pleaded softly. "Is it safe for me to visit?"

Afraid that the conversation for the benefit of the cavalry officer was sounding a mite peculiar, R. J. continued loudly, "Too bad you don't have a supply of 'shine with you to sell hereabouts, Ahab. Lots of troopers hereabouts, up to Athens and so forth. Why there's even a mess of them camped on Jesse Dodson's place . . . and more of 'em comin' down from the north every day."

The creak of the stairs out in the store warned us that someone was indeed coming down. To seem as relaxed as possible, R. J. and I picked up our coffee cups and wandered out of the kitchen. I got the shock of my life . . . all the accumulated debris of generations was gone! Even the fishnet and the ladies' unmentionables. "Yes, sir," R. J. remarked conversationally. "It sure is fine having so many of our brave boys around here. Why they think of uses for almost anything . . . even made springs for their cots out of old corsets!"

A pair of riding boots and pant legs of faded and indeterminate pale blue stomped into view from above. These were followed by a saber tip bouncing unsheathed from step to step and then the sleeve braid and collar tabs of a First Lieutenant, Confederate Cavalry. The short, beady-eyed officer was bald to about the middle of his head, but wore his remaining brown hair long and shaggy and tucked haphazardly behind his ears. "Well, Mister Ferguson, who might this be?" he demanded.

"Ah, Lieutenant Clark, this here is old Ahab from up Hiwassee way."

"You look able-bodied," Clark asserted. "Why aren't you in the army?"

Why not, indeed? What could I say to this suspicious little man?

"Say, Ahab," R. J. interrupted. "What was you telling me about Yankees over on Walden's Ridge?"

Bless R. J. Ferguson! If there was one thing this Reb officer could profit from more than a hillbilly recruit, it was information about the enemy! "Yessuh," I avowed. "Powerful number of blue bellies sweepin' over the hog-back."

His attention diverted, Lieutenant Clark demanded, "How many is a powerful number . . . one regiment, two? More?"

"Oh, my stars, Captain," I said, deliberately raising his rank, "there's a tremendous more than that. Must be forty or fifty thousand men the other side of the river. And horses! Ten thousand cavalry if they's a dozen. And such guns! Why Joshua would not have needed no trumpets if he'd a'had sech guns! Yessuh, nothin' gonna stop them Yankees short of Chattanooga."

"By thunder, General Forrest will give them a tune to dance to!" Clark declared. But for all his bravado and pride in his commander, Clark still looked ready to dash off and report. "Much obliged for the lodging, Mister Ferguson," Clark said. "Duty calls!" and the lieutenant strode out into the morning, yelling loudly for his sergeant to saddle up, they were to move out at once!

When we were alone, R. J. said, "I'm right sorry, Jesse, but I guess you got the gist of what I was tryin' to tell you before. Alcie's got a rough row to hoe and no mistake, but there's no way you can get over there to see her. Not now, no way."

"It's all right, R. J.," I said. "When you see her, tell her I'm nearby and that I will see her soon."

<hr />

Despite my concern about getting back across the river, I could not leave Tellico Junk right away. My disguise might work from a distance or in the early light of day but would not fool anyone who knew me. If a neighbor recognized me, I would be putting myself and perhaps my family in danger.

So I holed up with R. J. most of the day. He fed me

and filled me up with tales of Reb foraging and how any antislavery sentiment was likely to get a man arrested. Three times during my visit he hid me in the cellar when folks came calling, then drew me out again after the danger passed.

Finally I could not stand to wait any longer. Truth was, I feared that my troop would be getting antsy over my continued absence and might do something stupid.

So with the sun still a hand's breadth above the hills, I took my leave of Tellico Junk. Although I was concerned for Alcie and the children, I had learned that they were still all living, and that my joining the Union side had not caused them to be put off the farm. I had also gotten the information the army needed: Rebel General Bragg was pulling his troops south from the upper reaches of the Tennessee River and having them fall back toward Chattanooga.

Now to get back across the river to safety.

I sauntered casually along the main road till I came to where the dim outline of the disused wagon track branched off toward the mill. Passing by the turn without so much as a glance in that direction, I continued on a ways before pausing. Loitering in the shadow under an oak for a spell, I kept an eye on things till I was convinced there was no one watching me.

When I got to the knoll in the bend of the creek below the mill, I stopped and gave a bobwhite whistle to let my friends know that I was coming in. It came to me that Dobbs might be on guard and this might be the one occasion when he would actually hit what he was aiming at.

Instead of Dobbs it was Hamilton at sentry. He waved me in without a word and continued his watch.

"How'd it go?" Cochran demanded. "Any trouble? Can we head back now?"

"Simmer down," I told him. "Everything's fine, but we can't leave before dark. You know that."

"Sorry," he said. "I'm just all nerved up since those horsemen came by."

"What horsemen?"

Blanket explained. "Rebs. Joost thirty minutes ago. I was on guard when I hear harness jingle . . . I think maybe three or four riders."

"Did they see you?"

The German shook his head emphatically negative. "They did not come so far up as the mill. I only catch a glimpse off them down at the ford below. Three mounted men, like I figger."

"Where did they go?"

"Up the gully acrost the creek, und then I lose them in the trees."

My mind was racing. It could be Lieutenant Clark and his men, or it could be another Reb patrol altogether. Either way, it had passed entirely too close to our hiding place for my liking, and it was a long time till sundown.

There was nothing to do but wait, but I wasted no time in shucking the disguise and getting back into my uniform. Lieutenant Clark struck me as one who would be real pleased to hang a spy.

A few minutes later I went out to relieve Hamilton. "Anything?" I asked.

"Nope," he reported. "All real quiet."

He was too right . . . it was too quiet. "How long has it been since you last heard that 'baccy bird?"

There was not even time for him to reply before the unmistakable noise of approaching horses interrupted. "Warn the others and then slip down to the bank," I ordered. "Keep our nags quiet and see that the cinches and bridles are all tight, case we have to make a dash for it."

Three riders appeared at the ford. They split apart on the far bank of the stream, with one rider remaining opposite to the mill and the other two crossing and coming toward me. This looked for all the world like they had reason to be suspicious of the mill and were going to encircle it.

There was still a chance that they would look the place over and then ride off. Because of the thick brush, even the rider on the far side could not get 'round the mill pond to where he could spot our horses. If everyone stayed real still and quiet . . .

But it was not to be. Hamilton, who had failed to note the signals of nature, could not keep himself in check any longer. His Sharps boomed, and the Reb across the creek whirled his mount and dashed behind the brush.

Our one chance now was to fight and win. If they

got help we were cooked. Dobbs and Cochran must have thought the same, because another carbine blasted out a window of the mill, and one of the riders bit the dust.

The two remaining Rebs returned the fire, booming away with dragoon pistols. When the man on my side of the creek shouted across, I could tell by his voice that it was Lieutenant Clark. He called for the other feller to join him, and the trooper jumped his mount into the creek.

Midway over there was another shot fired from the mill, and the horse flinched and dumped the rider off in the water. Clark triggered off one more round that smashed through the rotten boards of the mill, then swung his roan to flee. Two shots followed him, but neither took effect.

Just that quickly the Reb officer was around the bow of the creekbed and out of our view. My first thought was *Good riddance, and we will vamoose too.* But it would not serve; I had no way of knowing how close by reinforcements were. Clark had to be stopped.

Digging my boot toes into the dirt bank with short, chopping steps, I sprinted toward the top of the knoll. I reached the low peak in the center of the horseshoe curve just as Clark circled it below me.

My leap from the summit was not an elegant dive. In point of fact, I plunged into the air feetfirst. Effectiveness substituted for grace though when my boots struck the Reb officer in the shoulders and we tumbled to the sand in a heap. His pistol boomed once more and went spinning away.

Clark was a game little cuss. Even knocked half silly and with me atop him when we hit, he was still trying to draw his saber when I brought my fists together on both sides of his head. That ended his resistance for the time.

By good fortune the reins of Clark's bay horse had tangled in some willows near the creek, and I caught him easily. By the time I toted the unconscious Reb back around the bend, Dobbs, Cochran, and Hamilton were saddled up and ready to ride. They had caught the other horse as well and had a Reb private tied into the saddle and gagged. "Where's the third man?" I asked.

Dobbs shook his head. "Dead," he said.

"All right then," I said. "Daylight or no, we can't wait around here to see who might have heard all the shooting . . . and we're taking these prisoners with us. Can't have this lieutenant asking around after someone of my description."

When we headed out, I led the troop across the creek, then back across, then up the center a ways so as to throw off any pursuit. Next we rode hard up the slope between Tellico Junction and Athens till we came to where the dim outline of a deer trail forked. "You go on up the west branch," I ordered. "When you come to the summit there's a canyon on your right with water and cover enough to hole up in. Wait for me there."

"Where are you gonna be?" Hamilton demanded.

I pointed to the other fork in the thin path. "This

curls around to a spot where I can look over our back trail," I said. "I want to see if anybody is following us. Now get along with you."

I had told the truth about the path I followed. It did give me a chance to study the ground back the way we had come. What I had left unsaid was of a more personal nature, and no one's business but my own.

Reaching a place where the trees thinned and the game trail played out, I tied my horse to an oak. Bent low, I crept up to the brow of the hill just as the sun was dropping behind Walden's Ridge. The last yellow light was washing out of the oaks below me, but it still lit the hay field in the curve of the river.

My hay field.

The crest on which I lay was just above my farm. It was to this very spot that I had brought Alcie when we were courting. I had stretched out my hand and waved it over an empty landscape and vowed to fill it with good things o' life and a place of our own.

Below me and across the stream stretched the pasture that I had not seen for months. The fences that divided the fields lined up with the dark green triangle of the late summer garden. The arrow formed thereby pulled my eye to the barn and just beyond it to the white clapboard house with its climbing roses and surrounding porch.

My chest ached with the nearness of it . . . and then Alcie stepped out on the porch. As though my presence had in some way called to her, she shaded her eyes and looked all around.

I wanted to jump upright, shout, wave, and caper! I wanted to run down the hill to her arms and never leave again! With a catch in my throat, I forced myself to lie still as two of my little ones ran to Alcie from the garden to clasp her about the knees.

Of the Confederate soldiers I caught no sign, yet their absence made things harder for me and not easier. The temptation to go to my loved ones was strong, yet I could not. Not yet.

Thank God the light faded then from her face and hair, veiling the nearness of my longing. When Alcie shooed the babies inside and reentered the house herself, I shook myself out of my trance and crept back to my horse, vowing to get back as soon as I could.

Within the hour I rejoined the others, and I reported faithfully that there was still no sign of pursuit. From that point on we rode through brush so thick no one would figure a squirrel could penetrate it. Twice we hid in thickets while other riders went by close enough to touch, and once we had to backtrack near a mile to avoid a Reb cavalry patrol. At midnight we forded the river, and after being challenged by the sentries, were led back to our camp.

It was only three days later that I headed back over the Tennessee River. This time all of Company F was with me and a whole lot of other folks besides. "Rosecrans has crossed the Tennessee below Chattanooga," Captain Briant informed us. "Now that the Rebs know where the real attack is coming, General Crittenden believes that Forrest will be moved south today, toward Charleston."

Briant went on to explain that it was the job of our cavalry, including Company F, to get between Old Bedford and the road south. If possible, we were to prevent him from joining up with Bragg. At the very least, we were supposed to delay the secesh horsemen till Chattanooga had been secured.

Our objective for this move was a place called Jasper's Ford. Sitting atop the road south from Knoxville to Chattanooga, the place was also at a bridgeless crossing of the Little Hiwassee River. It was believed that if we set up at that spot we could deny Forrest the passage.

We drove off some Reb pickets that were standing sentinel on the road and invested the ford with about a hundred men. Since we were mounted troops, we arrived considerably in advance of the rest of the expedition, but we were expected to hold on till reinforcements arrived.

The September day was hot and dry. In contrast to the rain and mud of the Tullahoma affair earlier in the summer, the ground was parched to the point of choking dust. The ford of the stream was nearly all bare rocks.

The other contrast to my earlier campaigning was the fact that we were on the defensive. Dobbs was assigned to keep the horses for Cochran, Blanket, Hamilton, and me while we formed part of the skirmish line. The actual ford was just upstream of us.

For a couple of hours we exchanged a few shots with Reb pickets on the other side of the stream, but nothing very heated. In contrast to the lazy battle, the sun at meridian height was exerting itself to be stifling, and the air was still and oven-like. Lying back in the brush behind logs and dirt mounds made the presence of the trickle of the creek a terrible ordeal. The water in our canteens was soon stale. We could not refill them or help ourselves to a cool drink from the stream since to move from cover was certain to draw a bullet.

At noon we saw a column of dust rising to the north of us and sweeping closer like that cloud that went before the Hebrew children. Cochran believed it to be our reinforcements arriving, but I said no. "Has to be Rebs," I explained. "Look where it's coming from."

So it proved.

We saw the movement of horses through the trees on the far side of the creek, but nothing clearly. It seemed that there was not to be an immediate mounted assault. Within a few moments, however, the popping of sporadic musket fire increased in both tempo and volume.

We fired back, and I was soon lost in the rhythm of the drill for our carbines: Crank down the lever to drop the breechblock, blow the residue out of the barrel, load another cartridge, close the block, apply a percussion cap, throw up the weapon, fire, repeat. Overhead a cloud of blue-gray, acrid smoke settled into the streambed until nothing of the other side could be seen.

It was as if the smoke was our enemy and we were doing our level best to annihilate it.

Little aiming was ever done, apart from pointing the muzzle in the general direction of the foe. It was an article of faith that only constant firing would keep the enemy from gaining an advantage. Therefore, only speedy reloading mattered.

Bullets whistling above our heads and into the trees reminded me of my duty as a corporal. "Aim lower," I shouted to both left and right on the line. Even as I spoke I saw Cochran trigger off a round while lying half on his side behind a log. The barrel of his Sharps pointed skyward. "Lower!" I hissed.

Screams punctuated the clatter of gunfire as bullets somehow found targets. Three places to my left a man gave a sudden groan and threw up his gun as if suddenly deciding to quit the battle.

A dozen Rebs dashed forward to the center of the stream. In their gray uniforms, they first appeared to be only darker swirls in the smoke. Even when they came to within twenty yards of us, they remained unreal until all were shot down and fell screaming or moaning or thrashing or heavily silent into the puddles in the ford.

There was a lull in the fighting. The barrel of my carbine was too hot to touch, and I reloaded it carefully, then set it aside. The sound of men coughing from the fumes and dust and heat replaced the noise of gunfire.

Down the line came Sergeant Cate. "Look sharp," he warned. "Keep your heads down and keep your cartridges to hand. They'll be coming on strong this time. Don't fire till I give the word."

A line of black ants trudged over the rock behind which I sheltered. They had a regular highway from one side of the boulder to the other and were bent on moving house or something from the amount of twigs and dry leaves they were carrying. How could they be so oblivious to the life-and-death struggle happening around them? At first I was amused, but soon I was envious of their lack of concern.

A shell from a Reb cannon whizzed overhead, bursting in the trees behind us. Then another shell dropped in the creek, showering us with gravel. The third round burst upstream of us, right along the shoreline. One man had his leg torn off by the explosion, and two more were killed outright.

I heard brush rattling and turned to see the cause. Though Hamilton was gripping his rifle with both hands, he was shaking violently and the barrel was thrashing in the branches of a bush.

"Easy, Hamilton," I urged. "You'll be all right."

"Corporal," he said, "are you scared?"

"Yes," I acknowledged. "A man'd have to be crazy to not be scared."

Hamilton nodded and licked his lips, smearing the stains of the smoke around his mouth. "I haven't been scared before," he said. "I didn't think I ever would be. I didn't know what . . . what it would be like."

"Take it easy," I said again. "You'll be all right."

A loud wailing cry from the far shore sent a shiver down my spine and made me doubt my own words.

"Here they come again!" someone shouted.

This time the streambed to left and right was full of dark, shaped wraiths and not men at all. There were so many of them!

"Fire!" Cate yelled.

A volley from our weapons cut into the oncoming shapes, twisting them into even more grotesque forms. Then, from up the creek to our right, came a bugle call and the sudden thunder of hooves. A troop of cavalry was hurtling down on us, already on our side of the water.

"We're outflanked!" was the cry, and, "It's Old Bedford!"

"Fall back!" Cate ordered. "Fall back to the horses!"

Hamilton was already sprinting to the rear, his carbine forgotten in the brush. A bursting shell scored his face with hot iron, and he screamed and threw up his hands. Others were throwing aside their rifles in their haste to escape.

I fired once more in the direction of the pounding hoofbeats, then rose to go. "Come on, Cochran," I said. "Time to get."

He triggered off one more round, then stood to follow me. Something seemed to slam into him from behind, and he pitched forward and disappeared in the brush and the smoke. "Jesse," his voice called feebly from somewhere in the haze. "Help me."

I reached for him, calling, "Where are you? Cochran, where are you?"

"Help me," Hamilton moaned. "I can't see! Help me! Somebody guide me!"

"Jesse," Cochran's voice called faintly from the mist.

"Jesse, come on!" Cate demanded. "Get back now!"

"But Cochran . . . ," I said, knowing that I would never find him until the smoke cleared.

"Corporal Dodson!" Captain Briant's voice ordered. "Fall back to the horses at once."

The shapes of three oncoming Rebs loomed out of the smoke. I drew my Colt and loosed three rounds at them before I left Cochran behind and fled. Hamilton's arm was wrapped around my neck, but for all that he was still running faster than me, practically dragging me with him. His scalp wound had bled into his eyes, but it was not serious. I wiped his face with a rag, then knotted the cloth over his wound.

Forrest's horsemen pursued us from the ford. We had held the crossing for exactly one hour . . . that was all.

We retreated down the stream and up the slope on the far side, looking for the high ground and a place to turn again on the enemy. When we pulled up our horses on a timbered hillside, it took me some minutes to recognize it as the same vantage point above my farm as I visited only days before. There was the same garden . . . the same house. I hoped my precious ones were inside and safe. I wondered if I was to die within sight of my home and family.

"They'll come at us from both sides at once," Briant warned. "Form an angle here with the point down the hill. Dodson, you and Cate anchor the ends of this line."

We could hear the Reb bugle calls gathering the troops again. Like a pack of hounds when the cougar is treed, the enemy horsemen circled and swirled at the foot of the hill on which we perched. Soon they would come for us.

To the note of the bugles was added another sound: a crash of exploding shells and the deep, bass rumble of the cannons. The shouts of Forrest's cavalrymen turned to calls of warning as cannon fire dropped in their midst. Then I heard Nathan Bedford Forrest's voice shouting for his men to regroup and fall back. "On to Chattanooga!" he yelled. "There'll be plenty more Yankees to kill down there!"

The arrival of our army and a battery of artillery saved our lives. Old Bedford and his troopers were past us and undeterred in their move to reinforce the Rebs to the south of us.

I returned to the creek after the skirmish to see about Cochran. He was not there at all.

⟫◆⟪

I cannot say how Alcie knew it was me coming across the meadow. I was covered with the dirt, smoke, and grime of battle. My beard had grown out grizzled in the four months since last I had seen her. The horse I rode was lean and hungry. I could not spur him faster than a walk or he would have collapsed beneath me. And if the horse was thin and ragged-looking then, I was double the vision of hardship. I might have been any stray Union soldier come riding in to look for a meal at the farmhouse. But somehow my Alcie knew it was me a'coming from half a mile off.

I raised my field glasses as I crossed the creek. She was barefoot and her golden hair fell in wisps around her face as she carried a laundry basket from the kettle toward the clothesline. Stopping midstride, she raised her head as if she sensed something. I rose in my stirrups and waved my hat broadly. She dropped her burden and began to run toward me.

I heard her shout to the children, "It's your daddy! Oh, God be praised! Jesse! My own Jesse!"

I kicked the horse. He would not move faster. Leaping from the saddle I left him behind, covering the ground at a lope.

She was weeping with joy when she reached me. The children galloped along behind her. We met beside the well, and I was surrounded by the sweet embrace of my dear family.

Alcie would not let go of me and cried, "Oh Jesse, you've come home to us at last! How I've prayed for this moment!"

Loren, thumping me on the back in a manly way, said, "Will you stay a while, Father?"

In a chorus the little ones chimed in, "How long will you stay?"

"Are you home forever now?"

"Is the war over?"

Such eager hopes filled me with sadness. Alcie caught the answer in my eyes. She answered for me, "Your father cannot stay long." Then she searched my face and kissed me again. "How long, Jesse? How long will you be with us?"

I swallowed hard. "Only today."

The younguns fell silent at this terrible reply.

"Ah," Alcie managed. She took my hands and held her chin up bravely. "Look at you, Jesse Dodson. You're a sight! I'll heat some water. You'll not go back to fight the Rebs looking like a scarecrow."

And so she wasted no time in caring for me as she had in the old days. She shooed the younguns out and set Loren to tend my poor mount. As I soaked in a steaming tub, she shaved me and soaped me and scrubbed me like I was one of the babies. But I had not seen her in so many months that the mere touch of her hands awakened a hunger in me deeper than any need I had for food and drink. We passed a sweet afternoon behind locked doors, and she filled me up and made me wonder how I would ever say good-bye to her again.

Afterward, she lay against my chest and told me what it had been like without me.

"I know the Rebs were here," I said. "And I watched you from the hill."

"I felt your eyes on me," she said in a soft voice. "Your thoughts comforted me. Did you feel the nights I lay abed dreaming of you, Jesse?"

"I have not forgot my promise to you."

"What news of William?"

"No news."

"The Rebs have stripped the smokehouse clean."

"I heard as much."

"The livestock is gone. Trafalger went with them. Loren tried to hide him, but they found him out."

"I have eighty dollars in Union gold. Enough to feed you and the younguns till I get back permanent."

"R. J. has been provisioning us. Beans and cornmeal and such like."

"A good man, R. J. is. I'll settle the account with him before I leave."

"Where will you go?"

"Chasing Forrest again, I reckon. South."

"I want you to stay, Jesse. I need you to . . ." She began to weep again, and her tears nearly melted my resolve.

"Please, Alcie. I will break if you cry."

"I cannot help it. It is harder to think of you being gone again when I have you back for such a short time! It is a dream! Only a dream!"

I stroked her back and spoke quietly to her. "Then we will dream together, Alcie! We have tonight! Let's not waste a moment of it!"

This was the only pleasant night I had as a soldier in Mister Lincoln's army. Come morning, Alcie removed a box from beneath a floorboard. In it was a fresh, new uniform that she had stitched for me and a new pair of boots that she declared she had bought in case I came home for Christmas.

"I see you are not a private any longer. If there was time I would sew your stripes on."

But there was no time for that. I kissed her and the children farewell, not knowing if I would ever see them again in this hard world. I could not dream what heartache lay ahead for us as I rode away from my home and rejoined my unit that day.

<hr />

After the skirmish at Jasper's Ford, Company F was shot up enough that we were detached from our service to General Crittenden. Despite what I had told Alcie, we were sent back to the regiment at Camp Spear. Because of that decision, we missed the Union capture of Chattanooga, but we also missed being in the shellacking our boys took at Chickamauga.

Forrest again, just as I might have predicted.

General Rosecrans, maneuvering the jaws of the Union nutcracker around Chattanooga, forced the Reb General Bragg to withdraw across into Georgia almost without bloodshed. The Rebs could not afford to be bottled up in a siege as had happened at Vicksburg. When the Twenty-first Corps came down the Tennessee from the north and Thomas's and McCook's outfits crossed Raccoon Mountain from the south, Bragg up and fell back along the line of the Western and Atlantic Railroad.

All well and good. Chattanooga was secured. Then Rosecrans overplayed his hand. He set out in pursuit of the retreating secesh but with his forces divided and spread out over sixty miles of country.

It was Old Bedford's command that discovered the gaping holes in the Union line and Old Bedford again who led the skirmishing around Tunnel Hill and Ringgold.

Then, on September 19, it was Forrest's outfit once more that opened the fighting at Jay's Saw Mill and the Battle of Chickamauga was on. For two days of slaughter on the creek whose Indian name means "River of Death," Forrest's men pinned down the Union left flank and prevented reinforcements from arriving in time.

When a gap appeared in the Yankee front, Rebel General James Longstreet sent twelve thousand men pouring across and the Union lines rolled up like a carpet. Much of the bluecoats dropped their arms and fled, racing each other all the way back to Chattanooga.

The battle ended with the Union army still in possession of Chattanooga, but surrounded there and besieged. Afterward, both Union General Rosecrans and Confederate General Bragg were sacked from high command.

All of which had little to do with me. Before returning

to Nashville, we put our more seriously wounded men aboard the hospital ship *Morning Star*. Hamilton, Dobbs, and I were assisting with the loading of stretcher cases and amputees.

Hamilton and I carried a twenty-year-old soldier whose thigh bone had been hit by a minié ball. The shattered remains of his leg had been removed halfway between hip and knee. As we toted the soldier from the field hospital toward the gangplank, he was raving to an imaginary surgeon not to do what had already been done. "Don't take my leg," he moaned. "Don't want to live with only one leg. Don't cut it off!"

Hamilton shuddered and tried to look everywhere but at the wounded man. But turning away did no good; the broken remnants of humans were all around, everywhere he looked. In fact we passed a barrel overflowing with removed human limbs. One arm balanced upright, palm open, as if giving a friendly wave.

That was all Hamilton could take. Without warning he abruptly set down his end of the stretcher and puked over a rail fence.

"Here, now," urged a man in the uniform of a naval officer. "You'll have to do better than that, soldier. If it was you on the stretcher, you'd want those taking care of you to be made of sterner stuff, right?"

Hamilton nodded weakly and apologized. "It came to me," he said in a puny voice, "that it could have been me. If Jesse here had not led me away after I got blinded, it could have been me lying here . . . or worse."

The naval officer was about my height and stocky. There was a notch missing from one of his ears. He nodded his understanding and directed us where to carry the wounded man. When we reemerged on the upper deck of the side-wheel steamer, he introduced himself. "Rafer Maddox," he said. "I'm captain of *Morning Star*."

As Hamilton was pasty-faced and wobbly on his feet, Captain Maddox invited us to sit down in his cabin for a spell. "Can't have you falling overboard," he said to Hamilton. "Turning you into a patient would be bad for the morale of the other stretcher-bearers."

The captain's cabin was on the top deck, two rooms back of the wheelhouse. When we entered the spartan room, a blue and gold bird screamed hello and bobbed his head by way of a greeting. "I'm Scrimshaw," the bird announced in the voice of Captain Maddox. "How are you?"

"Scrimshaw there has been with me ever since I went 'round the Horn in the early days of the Gold Rush," Maddox commented as he handed the bird a bit of hardtack.

"Then he must be . . ." I did a little mental arithmetic. "He's at least twelve or fifteen years old. I didn't know any kind of bird, even a parrot, could live so long."

"Nobody really knows how long they can live," Maddox said. "Some of these jungle birds make it to fifty or sixty years . . . maybe more. Scrim here could outlive me." Maddox thrust a dram of something into

Hamilton's hand. "Drink that," he ordered. "It'll do you good. What outfit you boys with?"

Hamilton drained the amber liquid, coughed, and got some color back in his cheeks. I explained where we had come from and about the fighting we had seen. Hamilton reached for the bottle and refilled his glass without waiting to be asked.

Maddox nodded his understanding. "Heard about Old Bedford even way out in California where I hail from," he said. "They say his troopers ride like cavalry and fight like infantry and that Forrest thinks the proper way to defend a position is to attack first."

I agreed. "That all squares with what we have seen of him. If it was up to me I'd just as soon not see any more of him, ever."

"Not see any more war ever," Hamilton muttered, tossing back the rest of the drink in one gulp.

"Here," Maddox protested. "You were just supposed to sip that."

"Thought I could whip all the Rebs myself," Hamilton mumbled. "Gonna show all the hayseed farmhands how to fight! Yessir! Was gonna show ever'body what real so'jers were."

Maddox glanced at me with a curious questioning look. "Had he been drinking already?" he inquired. "He hasn't had that much here."

Shaking my head I explained, "He hasn't slept since the battle at the ford. Got a bellyful of fighting and seeing men shot to doll rags. Had to leave a wounded comrade behind. Other men in the outfit tell me he hasn't slept a wink since that day."

"Oh-oh!" Scrimshaw announced, dropping his cracker.

Hamilton's body leaned sideways on the small sofa, and his eyelids drooped. "Looks like he will now," Maddox observed. "What say I give you a hand with the stretchers and we let your friend catch forty winks?"

An hour later I roused Hamilton and the two of us rejoined our outfit on the docks. "Thanks, Captain," Hamilton mumbled.

"Don't mention it," Maddox returned with a wave of his hand. "God go with you. Mayhap we'll meet again."

CHAPTER 7

$\mathscr{O}$KOLONA
WINTER, 1863–64

 When we got back to Camp Spear, we found out that more than Cochran had left us: Melvin Long was dead. His wound, which had not bled much and was thought to be healing fine, turned septic. Lockjaw set in; he was dead in days.

Throughout the autumn of 1863, the Third Regiment remained on guard duty at Nashville and patrolled the railroads in the vicinity. Old Unconditional Surrender, General Grant, was appointed the top commander of Union forces in the west.

Grant replaced Rosecrans with General Thomas, then went on to reinforce Chattanooga and break the siege. The Confederates were beaten at the battles of Lookout Mountain and Missionary Ridge. Then, in December, General Longstreet led his Rebel army away from Knoxville and back into Georgia for the winter.

By the end of the year, most of Tennessee west of the mountains was free of Confederate control for the first time since the war began. But not east. I reflected that the old woman Cochran and I had encountered was right to be canny: The Rebs still held much of my home county.

Our nemesis, General Forrest, was everywhere or nowhere, depending on which rumor one chose to believe: He was wounded at Chickamauga (which was true enough), he was dead (not true at all), he was in East Tennessee with Longstreet, he had argued with his superiors and gone home to his wife, he had rebelled against the rebellion and set up his own kingdom in Mississippi and made himself emperor . . .

All of which possibilities enlivened campfire conversations as the cold of winter closed in on Nashville. But on guard duty my solitary thoughts were still on home and on my son William.

I sometimes received permission to attend prisoner exchanges. I would stand for hours waiting in the relentless rain that came again to Tennessee as two hundred wretched Confederates would shuffle across the lines and two hundred of our boys, thin and ragged, would shamble back toward our side. I went from gaunt face to meager frame, studying intently each form. Never did I find William nor encounter any who knew of him. Still I kept trying.

The only campaigning done by the Third Tennessee Cavalry Regiment was in late December, right before Christmas. Nathan Bedford Forrest, despite all hearsay to the contrary, was truly raiding into West Tennessee, blowing up bridges, tearing up track, mustering recruits, and rounding up Confederate deserters for enforced reenlistment. The response of our commanders was to send us southwest to intercept him. We were part of a five-pronged attack designed to surround Old Bedford and end his depredations once and for all. Since there were fifteen thousand of us opposed to Forrest's estimated three thousand, our prospects looked fair to finally waylay the gray ghost.

We received our orders to move out on the eighteenth of December. For the first part of our journey we loaded our mounts into train cars (and ourselves as well—eight horses or forty men to a drafty, unheated carriage). Traveling down the line from Nashville we unloaded at Columbia on the Duck River and then went overland across the Tennessee River into the west. Three days later we were in position.

Forrest had set himself up a command headquarters at Jackson. He was reported to be fleeing south toward Mississippi with his three thousand men, captured weapons, looted stores, and two hundred head of cattle. Surrounded as he was, and with the rivers swollen and the bridges guarded, we thought we had him trapped for fair.

It was on Christmas Eve that our company went racing ahead of the foot soldiers to a crossing of the Hatchie River south of Jackson. The rain had stopped and a blue-cold moon hung over the bare branches of the oaks. Beyond the encircling trees stood a field of cornstalks, frozen stiff like a harvest of bayonets.

Owing to the sudden freeze after so much rain, all

the tree limbs were glazed with ice, and every puddle was a glassy slide to trap the unwary.

The men were huddled around fires, alternately squeezing close to the meager warmth and standing up to pound their fists on their shoulders and stamp their feet to get the blood going. Dobbs made an attempt at singing Christmas carols, but the response was halfhearted at best. It was too cold and thoughts of home and Christmas made the lonely night worse somehow.

Along about midnight, our infantry regiment arrived, about six hundred of them, and encamped next to us.

As corporal of the guard, I walked the rounds of the picket posts. As I approached Blankenbeckler's position there was an alarm. Outside of camp, off in the darkness, came a sharp snap like a single rifle shot. I snapped back the hammer on my carbine and was already racing forward as Blanket called, "Corporal of the guard, post nummer eins . . . I mean, one, one!"

The German was staring intently into the dark shadows cast by the moon and jumped when I touched his shoulder and drew him to a kneeling position. "Hunker down here," I whispered softly, "and listen for a minute. Frozen twigs will crack underfoot if anything much moves out there."

After some time passed without further noise, another sharp report again alarmed the sentries. This time the sudden noise was succeeded by a dull thud.

"Tree branch breaking from the weight of the ice," I said. "I'll pass the word."

Two hours later I was off duty and huddled inside a miserable shebang made of two shelter halves buttoned together. Dobbs and I were curled up in the dog tent, with one gum poncho under us and another over us and still not enough warmth between us to melt a pat of butter.

In the extreme cold, I was in a half-waking, half-dreaming state. I vaguely heard a further change of the watch, then somehow imagined I was at another prisoner exchange. Peering into every face that passed, I despaired of finding William. Each returning prisoner looked me in the eye, seemingly as eager as I to find someone who would care about him. Then to my vision was added a new distress: I believed William had already come past me and I had not recognized him! I frantically raced up the line, calling his name, then could not recall where I had left off looking. I panicked and pleaded with the captain not to load the men in the wagons just yet, that I had to find my son.

The officer in my dream opened his mouth to reply, but what he said made no sense. "Brigade—Charge!"

I woke with a start to find that the alarm was real even if the dream had not been. "Regiment—Charge! . . . Company—Charge!" The order was repeated down through the chain of command as out on the icy plain bugles blew and there came a sudden crashing tramp as of the boots of ten thousand men. A rattle of musket fire crackled down the length of a quarter-mile-long line of battle.

"Fall back," ordered the infantry colonel, a man named Prince.

"Wait," I heard Captain Briant argue. "We don't know what's out there. Let my men scout before we up and skedaddle."

"Are you deaf?" demanded Prince. "There are just six hundred of us here, and that's a full brigade out there . . . three thousand of them." Another clatter of gunfire swept down the line, and a few bullets whizzed through camp. "We've got to pull back!" Rebel yells from half of the compass pierced the stillness of the night. "There, you see?" Prince wailed. "We are about to be surrounded . . . we are pulling back at once, and your troopers are to cover our flank on the march. Do you hear me, Captain? At once!"

By five of the clock, Christmas morning, we were ten miles away at Somerville, where the presence of a bigger Union force stiffened Prince's backbone. All morning we waited for the command to ride out, to challenge Forrest, to deny him the road, but it was not until near two in the afternoon that Company F rode off toward Lafayette on the Wolf River.

We reached a covered bridge at dusk, a bridge that was supposed to have been destroyed to keep the Rebs from crossing. Instead the planks had merely been stacked and then left unguarded. Secesh infiltrators had tiptoed over the naked beams, relaid the flooring, and Forrest and his men had already crossed.

Company F was dispatched south at high speed to attempt to overtake the Reb column, though what we were supposed to do if we caught them was beyond me. We had not ridden above a mile when a shot rang out. I thought immediately of the snipers up on Calfkiller Creek and ordered my men to dismount and stay back of cover till we had located his whereabouts.

No more shots came. When Dobbs, Blanket, Hamilton, and I advanced again with our carbines at the ready, a lone Rebel lieutenant stood upright from behind a dirt bank and raised his arms. "I give," he said. "Only had but one bullet anyway."

"Why'd you stay behind then?" I asked suspiciously, scanning the surrounding woods.

The Confederate soldier looked chagrined. "Busted my ankle when I slipped on some ice, so I dropped out so as not to hold up the others."

As it was then dark, we took the solitary prisoner back to infantry headquarters. Colonel Prince had a nice, warm cabin in which to interrogate him. "Whose regiment are you with?" he demanded.

"Forrest's," was the proud reply.

"Yes, that's the brigade commander," said Prince, irritably. "But what regiment?"

That Reb junior officer laughed right in his face. "Guess it don't hurt nothin' to tell you now," he said with a smirk. "Last night . . . in the cornfield . . . there weren't no brigade. Gen'rl said if we couldn't sneak up we'd get louder instead. Shoot! Weren't even a regiment. Old Bedford had all of us repeat every command like we was forty companies, 'stead of just one."

"One?" Prince asked with alarm. "One company? Clear this room at once," he demanded, forcing Captain Briant and me out of the farmhouse.

We left, but not before we heard the prisoner say, "I declare, Colonel, there warn't but sixty of us! But the way those cornstalks snapped like gunshots, you must of thought we was thousands all firin' at once and comin' on like billy-o!"

⟫◆⟪

We did not get back to Nashville. Instead, after the failed attempt to corner Forrest in West Tennessee, it was decided to keep us there to guard against future raids. Hamilton remarked that such strategy was locking the barn door after the horse was out, and no one disagreed with him at all. First we were in Memphis, and then shortly after that were moved to Colliersville on the rail line, hard by the Mississippi border.

That winter was pretty much the coldest ever known or heard tell of in those parts. When we came back from riding patrol we could not dismount on account of our legs would not bend, not our backs either. We had to sort of fall out of the saddles and hope that the hostlers catching us were not themselves too stiff to manage it.

At first we were still housed in dog tents, but when it appeared that we would be staying all the cold season, we cobbled together all manner of contrived shelters. We built shanties, log huts, brush arbors, and most everything else we could think of that would be some protection against the cold.

Dobbs, Hamilton, Sergeant Cate, Blanket, and me had a prime stockaded tent. It came about this way: We offered to build Captain Briant a sturdy log cabin out of the sparse material available if he would let us take over his tent in exchange. He agreed, and both parties felt like winners. (Especially since the cabin turned out so nice that some other officer would have demanded it from us poor enlisted men if we had not made the deal beforehand with Briant.)

Our tent likewise finished up proper, it being roofed with vulcanized rubber ponchos and half-walled with sticks. We even caulked between the sticks with mud, but it rained so much we had to replace the chinking about once a week.

Anyway, on the tenth of February we were snug in our tent and had a fire going on our stone hearth and fireplace. The stones had been liberated from a Rebel back fence. We had likewise foraged for some empty barrels as had lately contained salt beef (called "old horse" by us seasoned veterans). By knocking out the ends and stacking the barrels one atop the other, we made a passable chimney. Our flue drew all right so long as the wind was not above five miles an hour. With any more breeze than that the fumes reversed themselves and turned our lodging into a smokehouse.

Dobbs was cooking for all of us. We were taking turns doing mess duty, and it fell to Dobbs to prepare supper. The regiment had received a fresh beef allotment that day, much appreciated after the run of salt pork and army beans that had been our fare for weeks. Dobbs was very proud of his ingenuity. He had located a store of onions and then traded some of them for pork fat in which to fry up the beefsteak and onions.

The fat was sizzling in the fry pan, and our mouths were beginning to water when all at once the bugle sounded. It was so unexpected that we all jumped up, including Dobbs who had been squatting near the cook-fire. His long-handled fork caught on the grip of the fry pan, upsetting the load of grease into the flames.

With a rush and a roar, the fat exploded up the chimney, which, being made of wooden barrels, likewise erupted into blaze! In moments our chimney was a conflagration.

Now chimney fires in winter camp were not uncommon. The usual practice was to push the flaming barrels over with long poles, away from the tent, and then reconstruct the flue shortly after, barrels being readily available.

On this occasion, however, there was no opportunity

to extinguish the inferno. The bugle call that had roused us was assembly, and it was shortly followed by boots-and-saddles. We were going winter campaigning, leaving immediately, and not even a burning tent was permitted to disrupt the progress of the army.

Because of the ferocious blaze, we did not have any chance to gather more than a few belongings by grabbing our haversacks. All our other possessions went up in smoke, including our extra clothing and the gum ponchos that had been our roof.

"Where we goin', Captain?" Blanket asked.

"Mississippi," was the compact reply.

"Iss any warmer dare?"

Captain Briant looked at the fiery remains of our tent, then at Dobbs, and then back at the German. "We got Private Dobbs, don't we?" he said. "Maybe it'll get some warmer after we get there." To the laughing and jeering that responded, Briant added, "And we want to make it real hot for the Rebs . . . we're gonna burn us down a Forrest!"

⟫◆⟪

It was not until we were on the move that we found out about our destination and the plan that called for such sudden action. General William Tecumsah Sherman, newly appointed commander of Union forces along the Mississippi, intended to strike a blow into the heart of Dixie.

Sherman would personally lead a twenty-thousand-man infantry force from Vicksburg overland toward Selma, Alabama. To defend his flank, seventy-five hundred cavalry troopers, of whom I was one, were to take off southwest from Colliersville toward Okolona, Mississippi, and then down the line of the Mobile and Ohio Railroad. The two converging columns of foot and horse would unite somewhere around Meridian.

Commanding the cavalry force was Brigadier General William Sooy Smith.

It was the common belief of Sherman and Smith that General Forrest could not successfully face two parallel threats into Mississippi. If the attacks were launched without preamble in the dead of winter and, as Sherman put it, "with celerity," there would be no opportunity for the Rebs to set up a defense.

At least, that was the reasoning.

We soon found out that though our tent had burned, we were not much worse off than the other men. No one was allowed extra belongings on the march. General Smith had ordered speed, which meant five days' rations per man, another five days' rations to follow by mule, spare horseshoes for each trooper, and nothing else except what would fit in a haversack. There would be no wagon train to encumber the columns of horsemen. Even the twenty cannons accompanying us were hauled by double teams of draft animals to defeat the Mississippi mud.

The other reason for the sudden haste was that we

were late. Unbeknownst to us in the companies, General Smith had delayed our launch until another force of Union cavalry joined us from Memphis. By the time we actually heard, "Column of twos. Comp-nee! Forward . . . Ho!" Sherman was already in Meridian, wondering where his cavalry had got to.

We rode for six days through some of the meanest country on God's earth. "Where are we?" Hamilton wondered aloud.

"Tippah County, Miss-sippi," I explained.

Hamilton looked around at the abrupt, treeless knolls and the clay-filled canyons and muttered, "What holds the cabins and the barns up on the hills? Looks like a light rain would wash them into the creeks."

"Often does," I agreed. "Folk hereabouts teach their cattle to swim before they turn them out to graze."

Hamilton looked at me to see if I was joking, then added, "I know you're joshing me, but tell me this: Why do we want this country? Seems to me we'd do more harm to the Rebs to make them keep it."

Everything about that land was mud-colored. Houses seemed to have been whitewashed with brown clay, and the sheep and chickens were somewhere between gray and tan. Even the folks thereabouts were all coffee-colored, and it was the white folks we was looking at. A line of laundry hanging between a sway-backed shanty and a leaning outhouse may have been clean, but the ragged pieces of cloth were universally ochre-hued. The onlookers we saw appeared to all be gray in their outlook on life too: None loosed a round and none waved to cheer us. Life was too hardscrabble to care much one way or the other who was passing by.

It was that same way clear to the crossing of the Tallahatchie River: no opposition at all. We were deep in Mississippi without firing a shot. It made me wonder where Old Bedford was; made me nervous. I only hoped it made our officers that way too.

By the nineteenth of February we were beyond Pontotoc, and both the scenery and the attitudes had changed. The muddy bottoms and steep defiles were replaced with rolling prairie, fertile and farmable and waiting only the kiss of spring to burst into exuberant green.

Exuberance among part of the population did not require the warmth of spring to bloom; the slave population, that is. South of New Albany we began to pick up contrabands, runaways from the plantations we passed. By the time we reached Pontotoc a full three thousand souls followed in our train.

General Smith fretted and fumed, appealed and decreed, but no amount of words, kind or otherwise, could make them leave off following us. Their presence pretty near doubled the size of our column; stretched us out, slowed us down. But how could we run them off, or run off and leave them?

These were not freedmen with homes of their own to which they could go. This was not Nashville, safe for runaways because of the protection of fifty thousand men in blue uniforms.

Until just days before, every man, woman, and child of the multitude now traipsing after us had been a slave, liable to be bought and sold, lost in a card game, beaten on a whim, or worked to death as the owner chose. No matter that genteel Southerners might protest that the Negroes were incapable of caring for themselves; no matter how much Rebels might argue that no right-minded slave-owner abused valuable poverty . . . regardless of high-sounding words and pat arguments, slavery was a great evil—the great evil of America. If slavery was not put away once and for all, then the Union did not deserve to exist.

If freedom was not important even to folks who had never tasted it, why did they leave the only homes they had ever known and what little possessions they had to cast their lot with us? They had seen, lived with, and tasted the dire consequences of revolution against their masters. They knew there was no going back.

I thought about the runaways who had crossed my land. I remembered Cyrus and old Samuel. But I saw the war in a new light down there in Mississippi; it had a different face. Before the war I had believed slavery to be wrong, but I had not gone to war to stop it. No, I had gone to war to find my son and to be able to live at home again in peace and safety.

Now, three thousand souls danced for joy when we came. They shouted "Glory!" and "Hallelujah!" They cried out praises to the Lord God Almighty, for "Massa Linkum's sojers." It made me frightened for them. They looked to us for protection and liberty, and we were taking them *south*!

There was a huge bonfire whereon a whole ox was being roasted. Hundreds of black men and women, who one day before had toiled on plantations under the watchful eye of their overseers and the threat of the lash, gathered and sang! They danced, clapped, and prayed, but most of all, they sang. Over frozen fields, filling the frosty skies, "Roll, Jordan, Roll," reverberated, and then we heard,

> Oh, freedom! Oh, freedom! Oh, freedom over me
> And before I'll be a slave, I'll be buried in my grave
> Go home to my Lord and be free!

Finally, to my amazement, they joined hands, and in a prayerful tone, with more feeling than I had ever heard applied to the words before, they sang,

> My country, 'tis of thee.
> Sweet land of liberty,
> Of thee, I sing!

This from folks who had never had a country to call their own before, or at least not one that meant anything kindly to them and theirs. It made me both proud and humbled at the same time to be wearing the blue uniform; to represent *freedom* to those folks. I could not work it all out, somehow.

<hr>

It was on the morning of February 21 that the whereabouts of Old Bedford once again became clear. After ten days of no opposition to speak of, Rebel skirmishers falling back whenever more than one company of us appeared, suddenly everything changed. As Hamilton said, "We got him right where he wants us."

What he meant by that was this: The cavalry column was way south, near the town of West Point on the rail line. We were smack-spraddle between Sakatonchee Creek and the Tombigbee River. The country on both sides of the tracks was swampy bottomland; good for hogs and cane, bad for horsemen.

"We can't maneuver off the roads," Colonel Minnis fretted to Captain Briant in my hearing. "We have them outnumbered four to one, but it doesn't count for a thing if we can only approach in a force that is twelve men across!"

To his credit, General Smith figured out the same thing and swore he would not let his command march straight into a trap. We received orders to attack the Rebs holding the bank of the Sakatonchee at a place called Ellis' Bridge. The purpose of the assault was not to force a crossing, but rather to disguise a retreat back the way we came.

"No heroics, Jesse," Cate urged. "We don't even want this piece of land, so don't go getting yourself killed."

I assured him I had no such intention. "I learned my lesson long ago," I reminded him. "You won't catch me doing nothing heroic."

In any event, the Rebs made it easy for us not to capture the bridge. Before we had come within twelve hundred yards, they opened up on us with a battery of six-pounders. Shells burst overhead, not doing any harm at such extreme range, but putting us on notice.

"Dismount!" Captain Briant ordered. "Every fourth man to hold the horses. Advance on foot."

Leaving Blanket with a fistful of reins, we spread out in a skirmish line a couple hundred yards across. From culvert to ditch we went, through a slough deep with slime, until musket volleys from the Rebs pattered in the branches like rain. "If they can do that, then so can we. Give it to 'em boys!" Cate ordered, and we opened fire.

There were some secesh pickets still on our side of the water, but when they saw our line of men approaching, some of them turned and ran. That was how I got another glimpse of Old Bedford. One Reb sentry threw away his rifle and sprinted across the bridge just as I cautiously poked my head up among some brush. About thirty yards the other side of the river I saw a high-foreheaded officer spur forward on his black horse and deliberately knock his own man down. The officer jumped from his mount, yanked the deserter to his feet, busted him backward again with his fist, pulled him upright once more, spun him around, kicked him in the behind, and gave him a shove back toward the battle line. I was so astonished I forgot to raise my rifle till the scene had played out and the moment had passed.

"Pass the word," Sergeant Cate called to me. "We've driven in their pickets. Hold here now."

I relayed the command to the others, then, in a lull in the shooting, had time to tell Dobbs what I had witnessed. "Saw how Old Bedford trains his recruits."

"Too bad you didn't give him a lead ball salute," he replied. "Him and his brother too." General Forrest's younger brother, Colonel Jeffrey Forrest, was reported to also be in the fighting that day. "Be something to ground sluice a brace of Forrests, eh, Jesse?"

After about two hours of no further real fighting, our regiment was told to withdraw. We had made enough of a show. I do not know how General Forrest knew what was afoot, but no sooner had we begun to fade back toward the main body than he launched a cavalry charge across the bridge. The sporadic staccato popping of muskets was replaced with a thundering rumble as the horsemen clattered over the wooden planks.

"Fall back!" Briant ordered. "Back to the horses."

Sergeant Cate and I covered the withdrawal, shooting into the oncoming riders and tangling up the front rank of what were now the attackers. Then we also turned to go.

Cate fired a shot from his carbine, then jumped atop

a levee to see if we had left anyone behind. That was when the Reb cannon opened up again. A blast into a water oak close behind the sergeant blew him head over heels into the river, and when he surfaced he was floating facedown.

There was not even time for conscious thought, so I take no credit for doing anything courageous. Courage, I have heard it said, is when there is time to think about not doing something fearful and then doing it anyway.

At any rate, I tossed aside haversack and carbine without regard. My running flat dive into the stream would have impressed my own children, but that notion did not come till later either.

The icy water made me gasp. I surfaced and saw Cate floating away from me, downstream. Reb bullets tossed up splashes close to my head, so I ducked under again into the pea-green liquid. When I came up next I grabbed Cate's leg and towed him over to the cover of some willows that overhung the water. Once under the trailing veil of limbs, I tossed him over a low branch.

Pounding him on the back brought no response at first, so I pounded harder. At last he gagged and coughed, so my treatment was working. I thumped some more, even though I could hear Reb snipers calling to each other, "Did y'all see where they went?"

Finally Cate groaned and said, "Jesse, is that you?"

I acknowledged as much.

"Would you leave off thrashing me then," he said. "I believe you've busted me ribs."

We stayed under cover for the space of two hours, half in the water and half on the muddy bank. I would have been hard-pressed to say which was the colder. Cate seemed to have taken no hurt from the concussion, and both of us had escaped being punctured by Reb bullets.

Finally, we snaked up and over the levee, drawing no more than a lazy parting shot. By following the stream northward, we rejoined our troop. Blanket had volunteered to be part of the rear guard, so as to be nearby with our horses.

"Corporal Dodson, I thought I made it clear there were to be no heroics done this day," Cate chided, his teeth chattering.

"So you did," I agreed, sniffling. "Shall I throw you back?"

<hr>

We retreated all that afternoon and into the evening, stopping to fight brief skirmishes on the road. We were slowed considerably by the contrabands who were scurrying along ahead of us, but at least we did not leave them behind.

At one point, a few miles north of West Point, we again halted to regroup. It was not, at least not at first, General Smith's intention to completely abandon the mission. So we formed again in line of battle and waited for Forrest's brigade to come up. Soon enough they launched an assault against the front of our position, even though the place was heavily wooded and provided us with good cover.

The onslaught by the dismounted Rebs was so fierce that we had no time to think about why they were pressing so hard against a strong location, until we heard the fearful cries from the contrabands.

Old Bedford sent a detachment of his men on a hard ride all the way around our position to attack it from the rear. To come up to us, the Rebs first cut and slashed their way through the colored folks.

Fending off the onslaught at the front with cannon fire of our own, Colonel Strong ordered a surging counterattack on the single regiment behind us. We batted them aside after a sharp fight and continued northward.

In front of me on my saddle rode a small black child who had gotten separated from his mother in the fight. Behind me clung an old, white-haired man with a saber cut over his ear. Again and again he kept repeating, "Lawd, Lawd, deliver us from Ol' Bedford." I could not agree with him more.

It was near two o'clock in the morning when we finally halted again and made camp about four miles south of Okolona. We had retreated close on thirty miles, fighting much of the way.

Having seen no pursuit since midnight, we felt secure enough to throw out pickets and build fires. We were almost too tired to cook a meal, though we had not eaten in twenty hours.

I was chilled clean through and real grateful when Blanket left off reading his book to put a cup of coffee in my trembling hands. There had been no chance to dry out since my unplanned swim in the river, and now rain began to fall again.

Drinking about half the thick brew, I then crumbled a hardtack biscuit in the rest. Since I had thrown away my haversack, I had no spoon, but lifted the gruel to my lips and slurped.

Mid-slurp I saw the eyes of the child on me. I still had not located his mother, and I feared she was dead. "Here, son," I said. "Find a cup or a can, and I'll share some of this with you."

Wide-eyed, the child only stared, but I could hear his stomach rumble.

"Please, suh," offered the elderly black man, "if you don' mind, the chile and I can share that soup in dis y'ar cup."

"I don't mind," I said. "It's a mighty poor excuse for soup though." Shortly after that I drifted into a fitful sleep.

I was feverish and chilled at the same time. As I had no blanket I was huddled next to the fire, but I awoke to find a scrap of faded cotton jacket over me. It belonged to the old man. "Where'd he go?" I asked Hamilton, who was bent over a fry pan of sizzling bacon.

"Said he knew there'd be more fightin' soon, and he wanted to take the child out of harm's way."

"But his coat," I protested.

"Said God bless you and you keep it," was the reply.

It was not even dawn when the cry was raised, "Here they come!" and it was so. Forrest's hard-riding troopers had rested for no more than two hours and had overtaken us again.

We did not even try to make a fight of it there, but mounted up and rode through Okolona to a wooded hilltop. There we would make another stand and try to prevent our retreat from turning into another rout as had happened at Chickamauga.

Hamilton cursed once as we rode out ahead of the column, then apologized for the slip. "It's just that we had to leave so fast I didn't even get to eat," he said.

"So?" I inquired crossly. "It's only a hunk of bacon."

"It isn't the meat bothers me," he replied. "I just figure some Johnny Reb rode into our camp and is probably helping himself to it right now!"

<hr />

By dawn of the twenty-second day of February, General Smith knew that the upcoming battle would tell the tale of the Mississippi expedition. Either we would stand our ground and be able to reassert our presence in Dixie or we would be routed and go home in shame.

We troopers recognized the same fork in the road as well.

As for the contrabands, they had already seen the future and expressed their opinion with their feet. Before a drizzling sky had grayed into morning, our camp followers up and left. They were putting more miles between themselves and the return to captivity that would surely follow a Yankee loss.

We were on a rise called Ivey's Hill that gave us a spot for our remaining guns and a vantage point to observe our pursuers. Directly back the way we had come was a small group of milling horsemen. They were easily seen across the open prairie, and numbered no more than company strength. Hamilton remarked, pointing, "Old Bedford's escort?"

I nodded, loading the replacement weapon I took from a dead trooper. "Figgers that way. He pushes all his men hard, and the ones nearest him he pushes hardest of all."

Off to our left was another mass of gray uniforms. They moved about in the brush that obscured the banks of the Tombigbee River, so we could not judge their numbers. But they looked to be at least brigade force.

We also knew that there was another Reb column trying to come up on our right so as to keep us boxed, but they had yet to put in an appearance.

"So far we still got 'em outnumbered," Hamilton remarked. "You figure Forrest will attack anyway?"

Sergeant Cate nodded without hesitation. "You be looking to your cartridges and swab that barrel out again," he said. "And do it sooner rather than later, if you take my meaning." Because of the rain we could not keep anything dry; not ourselves and not our weapons.

"But Sergeant," Dobbs protested. "How can you be so certain?"

"It's his nature, me boyo," Cate replied, inspecting Dobbs's carbine and handing it back. "I heard it said that when he was a child he was thrown from a young horse into a pack of wild dogs that had been harrying the colt."

He had all our attention now. "Go on," I urged. "What then? And speak up; I'm having trouble with my ears."

Cate made us count cartridges before he would resume. "Forty rounds a man," he said. "You'll be wantin' all of them before this morning's work is finished. Now, as to Old Bedford: Far from being torn to shreds, his body lit on top of two of the biggest mutts. He grabbed up one in each hand and dashed their brains out. Scared the pack so bad they up and fled."

"So even when he's outnumbered . . ."

"Let me see those bayonets," Cate demanded. "Aye, that's his way; throw himself on the pack of his enemies and expect them to run. Forrest is blackhearted as they come, but never doubt his audacity."

At this point Hamilton chimed in. "The *New York Tribune* agrees with you, Sergeant. One of our boys, who was captured after the fight at Fort Donelson and later escaped, said he heard Forrest say to General Pillow, "Wal, now, Gen'rl, we caint hold 'em, but we cane shore enuff run over 'em.'" Hamilton's mimicry of a broad backwoods accent applied to Old Bedford made everybody laugh.

"Well, now," Cate said. "It is a fine thing when the likes of a great man like Editor Horace Greeley sees eye to eye with the likes of me!"

At that moment the accuracy of Sergeant Cate's judgment was confirmed. The cry of "Here they come!" scattered us to the leeside of a three-rail fence, our carbines cocked and leveled. "Don't be scared, men!" Captain Briant urged.

"I am not scared," replied Blankenbeckler, just as if Briant had spoken to him in particular. None of the rest of us paid any heed.

In full view over the prairie grass was a tall figure who trotted his black horse to the front of the Rebs. He stretched upright in his stirrups, removed his hat, and swung to face our lines while waving the hat in his right hand.

Our own six-pounder guns saluted their charge, throwing up gouts of mud and smoke. At each explosion we looked to see the attack waver and splinter. Instead each blast seemed only to propel the riders forward with greater urgency and in no fewer numbers, or so it appeared.

We gave one volley from our rifles as they passed the center of the field, and then the horsemen swept around to our right and out of sight. That Forrest was leading an assault on our flank was proven within moments as first our boys from the Second Tennessee ran into us shouting and scrambling. These were succeeded almost immediately by troopers from the Fourth Regiment who stumbled as they ran, throwing aside weapons and haversacks.

"Stand and fight, yellow curs!" Cate bellowed, standing up and knocking one deserter down. He thrust a weapon into the man's hand and bodily flung him against a fence post. "May as well be killed fighting right here," he stormed, "as go to running and be killed by me."

The wild-eyed private with the insignia of the Second Cavalry grabbed the split-oak upright and cried, blubbered. "They're rolling us up!" he moaned. "Let me go, Sergeant, please!"

"Form a line here!" demanded Captain Briant, storming along the fence. "Here! Right angles to the fence!" He grabbed two other fleeing men and forced them down, turned me sideways and said, "Corporal, you are the anchor of this corner." Then off he went setting others in place so that we formed a broad arrow shape with the point toward the sound of battle now sweeping toward us.

General Forrest's bodyguard was joined by the brigade under the command of his brother. The combined force of riders thrust along the fencerow, sweeping up Union soldiers like a farmer raking brush. Then the line they were following dipped into a small hollow before rising again to our knoll.

"Now!" Briant yelled. "Pour it into 'em!" Four cannons in our battery unleashed loads of canister, and the lead pellets coursed across the field like blasts from giant scatterguns. We fired volley after volley into the mass of horsemen and succeeded in breaking up the charge.

Opposite me and lower, but still in an exposed position on a cleared knob of earth, was the tall figure on a black horse that I knew to be General Forrest. I laid my rifle across the top rail of the fence. His back was to me, and I could not shoot him that way. The wait for him to turn seemed endless, until at last he faced around.

Heedless of the shouting, the smoke, and the cries, I drew down on the topmost button of Old Bedford's uniform. There was no wind, and the shot was just slightly downhill. I blew out all my breath, wheezed, then drew a lungful and held it as I tightened my finger on the trigger.

My gaze was so locked on the brass fittings on his jacket that I did not see the other rider gallop into my sight picture until the very moment I squeezed off the round.

The new arrival was in the midst of saluting General Forrest. His hand went clear up over the top of his head instead, and he toppled from his saddle.

I reloaded quick as I could, but when I drew down again on Forrest he was off of his horse and kneeling beside the fallen man. Then a new surge of riders coursed toward me, and I transferred my aim elsewhere.

When I next had time to look for General Forrest, he himself was galloping toward our position at the head of a small band of men. A Reb bugler was blowing charge like it was the last trump.

Forrest waved his saber over his head. Though I could not hear his voice, the contortions of his face told me that he was screaming at the top of his lungs.

"Get ready!" Cate urged unnecessarily, and then the Rebs were on us. Old Bedford put his horse at the rail not twenty feet from me. As he cleared the jump, Forrest slashed downward with his saber. The blade hit Blankenbeckler between neck and shoulder. The German gave a sudden shout and fell halfway through the fence rails.

I swung my gun to follow the attackers, squeezed the trigger and shot. General Forrest's horse screamed, reared, and plunged forward, then fell to its forelegs.

A cannon boomed close behind me, and a surge of smoke billowed over the scene, closing off everything more than arm's length away. And . . . I was out of ammunition.

Briant and Cate were both shouting for us to fall back, but I crouched and ran toward Blanket. He was dead, of course. From the front of his blouse had fallen his slim, leather-bound volume. I grabbed it up and then seeing myself about to be surrounded and cut off, I turned and ran.

Fortunately, the Rebs had not captured our horses, so those of us who were left, mounted and made our escape from Ivey's Hill. We retreated another thirty miles that day. I was stone deaf in both ears and fevered, but I stayed in the saddle some way or other.

That was much the end of the Mississippi expedition. General Smith reported that we made a "fighting withdrawal." Unsympathetic papers called it a "stampede." What I know is this: We went back to Memphis in half the time it took going. We never did meet with General Sherman's infantry, so he gave it up and turned back too.

Two more things: The man killed on the knobby hill while reporting to General Forrest was his brother, Jeffrey. The book that fell from Blanket's tunic was in German. Its title read: *Wie die Religion taeglich zu ueben sey*. It was not until some time later that I located how it translated: *How to practice religion in daily life*.

CHAPTER 8

ORT PILLOW
APRIL 1864

The shattered pieces of the Third Regiment were ordered back to Camp Spear in Nashville for the rest of the winter. Unlike our previous times in camp, there was little more drill. Morale was low. As Dobbs said, "We had been whupped for fair." There was no arguing the point, and it seemed that no one was likely going to give us a chance to redeem ourselves anytime soon.

Along about the middle of March, Sergeant Cate hunted me up and told me I had a visitor. When I came outside of our tent I found a slim but broad-shouldered, young black man waiting for me. He was wearing the red-braided blue tunic of a private in the light artillery. "Can I help you?" I said, thinking there was some mistake.

"Don't ya know me, Mistuh, I mean, Corp'rl Dodson?" he asked, grinning.

The familiarity in the voice made me look more closely at his face, and then, "Cyrus! Is it really you?"

The smile got even broader till it lit up the overcast day. "It shore enuff is me. Can we set a spell and talk?"

I invited him in, asking only that he speak up. I had regained my hearing in my right ear but was still having trouble with my left. I was also still subject to a recurring fever, but of this I said nothing.

Cyrus explained that after our meeting in Nashville he had wandered north, enjoying his newfound freedom but not knowing what to do with it. "Then it come to me what you said about giving back to the Lawd as He has prospered me," he said. "Well, suh, the onliest thing I gots to give is this'yer hide. So I says, Cyrus, you go on down and jine up and learn to sojer like Mistuh Jesse. And here I is."

He could not stay long as his outfit was moving out that very day. "But if'n you gets a chance, come see me at my new post," he said proudly. "Fort Pillow on the Miss-sippi River!"

It chanced that only a couple of weeks later I learned of a prisoner exchange to be held in West Tennessee, and off I went to look again for William. It seemed to those who knew me that I was chasing after an unlikely dream; the sensible thing was to give up hoping I would ever find William alive. After all, prisoners were able to write letters sometimes or to send word out to the families by way of those being exchanged. If William were still breathing somewhere, I should by then have known it. I recognized all this, but still I never gave up, and no one tried to talk me out of it neither.

Anyway, that was how I came to be on the Mississippi on the night of April the ninth. The prisoner exchange had been one day earlier at Hernando, just below Memphis. There was no William among the ranks of the ragged but elated Union soldiers, and I was fixing to hop a train back toward Nashville when a voice hailed me. "Hey, Corporal. Didn't we meet up back near Chattanooga?"

It was Captain Rafer Maddox of the hospital ship *Morning Star*. On his shoulder rode the blue and gold parrot, Scrimshaw. Maddox was in Memphis to transport some of the seriously wounded soldiers up the river to a hospital in Ohio.

We visited for a bit, and then he offered me a ride on the steamer. I declined. "Gotta get back to camp," I said. "I'll be catching a train in an hour or so."

"Haven't you heard?" he asked with some surprise. "Reb cavalry busted up the tracks in a raid between here and Brownsville. It'll be two days or better before your train will run."

I fell into a brown study, thinking how if I was late returning to Nashville, not only would Captain Briant skin me, he would never let me go off to another prisoner exchange. I said as much to Rafer.

"Tell you what," he replied. "Go with me as far as Hickman, Kentucky. You can catch a train there for Nashville."

After the *Morning Star* got under way, I found out that she was putting in at Fort Pillow to drop off some medical supplies. So it appeared that if I had met Captain Maddox again by providence, I was also fated to see Cyrus on this same trip.

Fort Pillow was forty miles overland north of Memphis and eighty by the loops and curls of Old Man River. Going up against the current, it was midday on the tenth before we drew abreast of the last bend below the fort.

There was smoke billowing over the headland, and when Rafer stopped the engine we could hear the sound of guns. Many another captain would have put the helm over and run for cover or idled up until he knew it was safe, but not Captain Maddox. He rang the engine room for full speed, reasoning that his was a hospital ship, and where there was shooting, she would be needed.

Around the bend we came in sight of the outpost. Fort Pillow was a small place, perched on the brow of the Chickasaw Bluff. It had but six guns and was defended by about six hundred men. It was so far up the river that no one thought it would be attacked seeing as the war had moved away south.

Once again the Federal commanders had reckoned without General Forrest. His way of defending by attacking carried over whether it was one battle or a whole campaign. Not content with having kicked us out of Mississippi, he had struck into West Tennessee. It had been his troops who cut the rail lines, and now they were assaulting Fort Pillow. Its capture would threaten Union shipping on the river.

When the steamer arrived, a Union gunboat was

blasting away at the ravines that lay on both sides of the fort. From our vantage point on the water, we could see that the shells were having little effect. Every time the floating gun platform maneuvered to lob canister at the Rebs, the graybacks moved around to the other canyon and continued the attack.

Up on the clay knoll the defenders were hard-pressed. The slope was so steep that they could not depress the guns in the fort low enough to sweep the ravines. Worse yet, Rebs had found high ground beyond the fort from which they could snipe at the men inside.

The fighting went on for three more hours or till about midafternoon. The Rebs gained the ground just outside the walls. Whenever the defenders leaned over to fire their rifles down, Reb sharpshooters would pick them off.

I saw a flag of truce go up to the fort from the attackers, and for a time the firing ceased. Whatever parley took place, Old Glory was not lowered from the staff over the walls, and the assault resumed, but the stalemate was over.

The Rebs stormed the walls, boosted one another up, and I counted near eight hundred Confederates achieve the top of the parapet. They jumped down inside, and I groaned in the expectation of surrender.

What followed was worse than any capitulation. As the Rebs poured over the walls, the defenders, mostly black men, streamed out the gate and tumbled down toward the river, just as the victorious Rebels tore down the U.S. flag.

But there was no surrender.

As Captain Maddox and I watched with horror, the Rebs surrounded men who had thrown down their guns and shot them! Even those whose upraised arms could be plainly seen were bayoneted to death or sabered and their bodies pushed into the river. I saw black troops fling themselves into the stream attempting to escape the slaughter.

The Union gunboat stood in toward the bank to try and pick up some of the survivors. Immediately, the cannons in the fort, now manned by secesh gunners, fired at the gunboat and drove it off.

On shore the massacre continued until a red stain floated with the current. For two hundred yards the Mississippi ran crimson with blood.

"Do something!" I pleaded with Captain Maddox.

The good captain needed no urging. *Morning Star* forged across the stream toward those floundering in the water. His second in command protested that using a hospital ship to rescue men in conflict was a violation of the rules of war.

Rafer backhanded his lieutenant and ordered him out of the wheelhouse. "Do you see that!" he shouted, his face fiery with anger. "Is that butchery according to the rules of war?"

Without further thought, Captain Maddox imposed the bulk of the steamer between the shore and the swimming survivors. Racing below, I helped pluck wounded and drowning men from the current.

I saw an arm wave and heard a gurgling cry for help; saw a soldier go under. As at the fight at Ellis' Bridge, I jumped without thinking into the water.

It was not Cyrus that I rescued that time, nor any of the three more times that I plunged into the muddy water. But Cyrus *was* plucked from the Mississippi that day, a bullet wound in his shoulder from where he had been shot in the back.

The Rebs took the cannon from Fort Pillow; they only held the fort for about a day before retiring, and the raid was over.

General Forrest was reviled in the Northern papers for ordering the massacre. His printed reply was that he had not ordered it but was incapable of preventing it. Forrest was not sorry. His statement in the Southern papers was, "It is hoped that these facts will demonstrate to the Northern people that Negro soldiers are no match for Southerners."

Cyrus went into the hospital. He lived, but he would fight no more after his first battle.

Fort Pillow had two personal consequences for me: The repeated immersions brought on a new bout of fever, and I lost what little remained of my hearing in my left ear. Also, I went no more to prisoner exchanges, because there were none. As a result of the atrocity, General Grant refused to exchange any more Reb soldiers.

Both the nation's conflict and my personal one had grown more bitter than ever.

⟾•◇•⟽

The regimental surgeon, Dr. Souers, waited for me to button my tunic and seat myself on a camp stool next to his desk. Despite his frequent recourse to that medication for all complaints, Doc Quinine did not this time offer me the familiar cork-stoppered brown bottle.

"Corporal," he said in a low voice, "you are a very sick man."

"What?" I said. "You'll have to speak up. I've gone deaf in my left ear, you know."

"I know," he agreed, moving to my right side. "I did that on purpose to make a point. You are stone deaf on one side, and you've lost about 25 percent of your hearing on the other."

"I'm better now," I protested. "Getting stronger every day."

"Corporal," he stressed again, "I may be an old country sawbones when it comes to modern medicine and such, but even I know the rheumatic when I see it. Besides the hearing loss, it's weakened your heart and lungs. Why you don't have consumption I'll never know. As it is, the first bout of camp fever may carry you off. At the very least any more sickness and you'll be deaf as a post for the rest of your life."

That brought me up short. I thought of not being

able to hear Alcie's sweet voice, the laughter of my children, the songs in church, the muted whispers of mornings in Alcie's arms before the children waked. It was hard. I hung my head. "What's the answer, then?" I asked without lifting my gaze, for I already knew the response.

"I'm sending you home," he said. "Given time, rest, and proper food and care, you may beat this thing. But not here; not under these conditions. Do you know how many men have been killed in battle since this regiment was formed?"

His question took me by surprise. "No," I replied. "Blankenbeckler. That lieutenant . . . ?"

"Eight," Dr. Souers said distinctly. "That's all. Do you know the number of good men who have died of illness or of wounds that should not have killed them?"

I made no reply.

He ran his fingers through his thinning gray hair and propped his sagging jowls on weary fingers. "We just don't know enough," he said softly, then repeated louder. "We don't know enough to save them."

"Can you make me leave?" I asked. "Isn't it my choice?"

Dr. Souers nodded slowly. "You don't have to accept a medical discharge unless you are endangering the lives of others. But why stay? Don't you have a family? Haven't you seen plenty of maiming and killing for one lifetime?"

"My boy William," I replied. "He may still be a

prisoner . . . or he may already be dead. Either way, I owe him. He was stronger of his convictions than me; a better man than me. Other good men, too: Long, Cochran. I owe it to them to see this thing through." My heart sank inside me even as I proclaimed the words. We had just heard that the Rebs had retreated from East Tennessee; I *could* have gone home again, and yet could not.

There was a long silence as the doctor and I regarded each other, then when he spoke again it was in a matter-of-fact tone. "Don't get chilled. Treat the least quinsy or fever as life-threatening, because it is. Stay warm and dry, or I won't answer for the consequences."

Nodding slowly, I thanked him and rose to leave.

He stopped me at the tent flap by mumbling something I could not hear. "What was that?"

"Four hundred thirteen," he said. "Fever, bloody flux, little scratches that didn't bleed a teaspoonful . . . four hundred thirteen from this regiment alone."

CHAPTER 9

*S*ULPHUR BRANCH TRESTLE
SEPTEMBER 1864

By late spring of 1864, the Union strategy for ending the war was at last being realized. General Sherman was moving to cut the Confederacy in two, from Tennessee to the ocean. In the East, Grant kept the pressure on Lee so that the Reb Army of Virginia could not go to the rescue of Atlanta.

Sherman's biggest worry was his five-hundred-mile-long supply line. Since it stretched from Louisville, Kentucky, clear through Nashville to Chattanooga and on into Georgia, a strong Reb force in Middle Tennessee could cut him off.

Everybody in blue, from the highest major general, to the rankest private, knew that Forrest was the danger. Who else but Old Bedford could move fast enough and hit hard enough to endanger Sherman's march to the sea?

So it fell to the Tennessee Volunteer cavalry regiments to counter that threat. During this time, I and the rest of the Third Regiment were still guarding trains out of Nashville, but we eagerly followed the news.

To begin with, just the Union troopers stationed in Memphis were enough to hold Forrest back. Sherman rightly guessed that General Forrest would not leave Mississippi undefended against another Yankee invasion, and that strategy worked for a time.

Then came June and the fight at Brice's Crossroads, Mississippi. Old Bedford whipped Union cavalry and then infantry, one after the other. The Union force went reeling back to Memphis, having lost six hundred men killed or wounded and nearly two thousand captured. Once more Negro soldiers were slaughtered, the number of dead from their brigade being greater than those from all the other five brigades combined.

If the fighting in Mississippi was again a disaster for the North, it at least accomplished its purpose. Forrest was unable to attack Sherman's railroad lifeline. Another Union invasion of Mississippi in July also resulted in defeat but again kept Forrest in check. It was God's own providence that the leadership of the Rebels preferred to keep Forrest back rather than unleashing him on Tennessee.

In mid-August Old Bedford shook up the Union commanders by launching an offensive of his own. He reasoned that if he could not cut off Sherman's supplies, the next best thing would be an attack northward that would force our generals to leave off attack in favor of defense.

So Forrest raided Memphis in the early morning hours. Despite the fact that the city had been solidly in Union hands for two years and was full of blue uniforms, Forrest's men achieved complete surprise and captured six hundred men.

At Camp Spear, on a muggy August night, those of us of Company F were discussing all these things.

"They say Forrest has fifty thousand men, and he's coming to attack Nashville," a wide-eyed new recruit named Friesen gulped.

Dobbs snorted, with the air of a seasoned campaigner who discounted ninety percent of any rumor he heard. "Old Bedford may be worth a lot," he scolded, "but to make up fifty thousand he'd have to count for forty-five thousand of them his own self."

"Won't Sherman have to turn back now?" Friesen persisted.

"Not a chance," Hamilton concluded. "But I do know this: Next time somebody gets up an expedition after Forrest, it'll be our turn again."

We thought that over with mixed emotions. I concluded that Hamilton was undoubtedly right. The Third Regiment had been out of the line for six months; our number was sure to come up again soon.

That night I wrote a letter home to Alcie. I proclaimed again my intention to keep my promises. I would still believe that William was alive, and I would live to come home to her. I made little remark of my ailments; it was little enough to do to spare her fretting. I could not resist telling her how much I missed her and ached to hold her.

Then, on September 2, Atlanta fell to Sherman's invasion, and the awakening at the end of the long nightmare of the rebellion was near. Too late the Rebel high command recognized the need to use Forrest on the offensive—too late to defeat Sherman, but not too late to involve the Third Tennessee in another campaign against Old Bedford.

It was reported that Forrest had moved his command to Cherokee Station, Alabama. If such news was true, it could only mean that he was preparing an assault north toward Nashville. We were dispatched to deal with him.

One thing of note occurred before our departure: Our trusty, single-shot carbines were taken from us and replaced with Spencer seven-shooters. "Load 'em in the morning and fight all day," Hamilton quipped. Other units had already been using the repeaters with the tube magazine that fitted into the stock. They were supposed to make one man fight like a company; a company like a regiment. Friesen said he felt invincible. The rest of us just hoped we would finally be able to lick Old Bedford, instead of coming back with our tails between our legs.

Once again we loaded into railcars and over the line of the Nashville and Decatur, were moved to Athens . . . Alabama. Not my home near Athens, Tennessee, but one hundred twenty miles away from there.

We rode out toward Decatur on the twenty-third of September and almost immediately had a skirmish with some Reb troopers. Sure enough, the Spencers worked like champs. The Rebs charged with their usual dash and clamor, but each time we were able to turn them back without loss to ourselves. After three tries, they drew off to reconsider, and we returned to the fort at a place called Sulphur Branch Trestle.

⟶◆⟵

"Did you ever see anything like that?" Dobbs questioned me. "Ain't that the biggest dang bridge you ever seen?"

I agreed with him that the wooden structure was enormous. Spanning a tributary of the Tennessee River, the trestle was over seventy feet high and more than three hundred feet long. It was of major importance to the line of the Nashville and Decatur Railroad. The platform was to be protected so as to allow our troops to move into Alabama, or, failing that, to be destroyed, so as to make it tougher for Forrest to move north.

As we were rubbing down our horses, I overheard a conversation between Colonel Minnis and the commander of the fort, Colonel Lathrop.

"Minnis," Lathrop said, "have your men stable their horses and draw ammunition. Then have them see Captain Pierce for their assigned positions."

"Assigned positions?" Minnis questioned. "Colonel, my men are ready to take the fight to the enemy. We can punch right through their line tomorrow or harry them until reinforcements come up."

Lathrop snorted. "How many men do you have, Colonel? Four hundred? Don't you know that Old Bedford is coming on with thousands?"

"Begging your pardon, then," said Minnis reasonably. "In that case, wouldn't it be prudent to torch the scaffold now and fall back on Pulaski?"

"From bravado to timidity so quickly, Colonel?"

I could see Minnis swell up and redden about the back of the neck. Our orders put him specially under Lathrop's command, so there was no arguing.

In any case, Lathrop continued, "Besides, Colonel, we can hold them off here! Look at the works of this fort. And what about your new Spencer repeaters? Let me show you around the walls, and we can discuss the defense."

"Did I hear the man?" Cate hissed in my ear. "Defense, he says! Sure, and I'd rather have a fine animal beneath me and a field crawling with Rebels in front of me, than be stuck in here!"

Straightening up from clenching horseshoe nails, I turned 'round and regarded the fort. The fortifications consisted of a pair of blockhouses made of railroad ties and a surrounding earthwork. "Them blockhouse walls are three feet thick," I commented. "Maybe the webfoot colonel knows his stuff?"

"And I'm Saint Patrick," mumbled Cate. "All right, then, Corporal Dodson. After the good captain lets us in on our positions, you and me will see how we can make the best of it."

We shared the defense of Sulphur Branch Trestle with two hundred Indiana cavalrymen and four hundred colored infantry. Together with our regiment, we totaled about a thousand.

Our company was detailed as part of the defense of the south wall of the earthwork. "Did you happen to notice something odd about this fort?" Hamilton asked, then without pausing, answered his own question. "No cannon. The platforms are in place, but there are no guns mounted."

"So?" I said cautiously, not wanting to broach my own concerns.

Hamilton looked me square in the eye. "Don't try that on me, Jesse Dodson, corporal or not. You see it as plainly as I do. If we have no cannons and Forrest does, we're in a quicksand bog up to our necks, and no mistake."

<hr />

Colonel Minnis suggested to Colonel Lathrop that we throw out a picket line outside the earthworks, even volunteered our company for the job. Our commander hinted that some advance warning of the arrival of the Rebs would be a good thing; said we might even disrupt their attack and make them draw back.

Lathrop refused. "Can't spare any of the defenders,"

he said. "Besides, if one of your boys got himself captured, he might shoot his mouth off about our defenses here. Can't have that, now, can we?"

So as night fell, we took turns about patrolling the six-foot-high berm around the compound. When we were not on guard, we sat beside small campfires on the sultry, warm, Alabama night.

"'Scuse me, Corporal," one of the Negro soldiers said to me. "Is you name of Dodson?"

"That's me," I admitted.

"Wal, my name is Private Fletcher, suh. My cousin be Cyrus, you know, him you save from out the river?"

"I didn't exactly save him," I confessed. "But I was there. How is he?"

"He doin' much better, suh. He still in the hospital, but he gonna be fine, they says. He tole me to watch out for you if'n I met up with the Third Tennessee."

I shook Fletcher's hand warmly, told him I was glad of the news about Cyrus, and expected the private to return to his post. Instead he hung about expectantly, as if there was more he wanted to say.

At last he spoke again. "You at Fort Pillow," he said. "You seen what the Rebs done there?"

"I did," I replied. "I won't ever forget it neither."

"And Old Bedford, he the same what comin' here?"

I allowed as how that was what we had heard. "Are you afraid?" I asked.

"No suh!" Fletcher said promptly. "I been wantin' a

chance to settle up with Gen'rl Forrest. Evuhbody in my outfit feel the same way too. Just wish . . ."

His voice trailed off into the starry Alabama sky. "Wish what?"

"Wish we outside, 'stead of waitin' in here. Don' know what kinda fightin' we gonna see."

I nodded my understanding. "Tell your outfit just to soldier like they know how," I said. "That's all any of us can do."

Fletcher nodded and left me then, but almost immediately Dobbs came over. "Jesse," he said, "you been my friend since I first joined up, and we fought a heap of battles together."

"That we have."

"Skull Camp Bridge, Jasper's Ford, Ivey's Hill," he called the roll of conflicts. "Anyways," he continued, then stopped. "Anyways, I want you to do something for me."

"Shore," I said. "What?"

"Hold these for me." He handed me a scrap of paper folded twice over. It was heavy. "My watch and chain," he said. "It was my daddy's, and if tomorrow . . . if tomorrow . . ."

"Don't talk like that," I urged. "We've come through tough spots before. Tomorrow won't be any different. We even got reinforcements coming down from Pulaski. We'll be fine."

Dobbs was already shaking his head before I had

finished speaking. "Promise me, Jesse," he begged. "See that my family gets it if I don't make it."

What was left for me to say?

"'Course," I agreed. "But you'll see. I'll be giving it back to you tomorrow night."

Later on, Hamilton asked me if I ever had any premonitions before a battle.

"Premonition?" I repeated. "You mean, forboding? I guess ever'body does some. Any time you know there's gonna be a battle, you can't help but think on it."

"How do you handle it?"

The last thing I wanted was to give a hackneyed answer to a serious question. Even though I was not an officer, lots of those boys looked on me as a kind of father, on account of my age. What would I say to my own son, if he had been in the spot we were in?

Finally the answer came. "Can you promise me that you will wake up tomorrow when you go to sleep tonight?"

"No," he admitted.

"Or testify that your heart will keep beating or that you will keep breathing after the very next breath?"

"You're driving at something, Jesse," he said. "Say it."

"None of us has a bridle on our own life," I said. "Doctor says I could die from catching a cold . . . wouldn't even have to stop a bullet, just a raindrop. So . . . man's gotta live as though he's ready to meet God any day or night. That way, it don't matter whether you think something's gonna happen or not. If I walk outta this skin tomorrow, or not for seventy years, the main thing is I want to be ready to see Jesus right after."

Nodding slowly, Hamilton acknowledged the reply. "Thought that's what you'd say," he asserted. "Just wanted to hear it directly from you."

There was a lot of praying and quiet hymn-singing in camp that night. We did not know what the next morning would bring.

———⟶◆⟵———

I do not think that anyone in the garrison at Sulphur Branch Trestle slept much, even though the night seemed to last a hundred years. When dawn finally winked a gray eye on the eastern horizon, every man was on the parapet, straining to see.

"There!" Hamilton exclaimed, pointing. "What's that row of dark shapes over there?"

Similar discoveries were made all around the fort. On every side of the compound, too far in the half-light to be clearly made out, were squat, black forms, like rows of obediently crouching dogs.

"Batteries," Sergeant Cate observed. "Moved 'em up all around us in the night."

Because of Colonel Lathrop's unwillingness to allow night patrols, our position was now ringed by guns, their open mouths gaping. We had no cannon of our own with which to reply to this peril. The Rebs must have known our predicament, too, because they had planted their batteries in plain sight.

"Too far for us to snipe at the gunners," Hamilton observed. "We'd best get up and charge 'em before they start throwing shot."

I agreed with that reasoning: Take a page from Old Bedford's book and defend by attacking. But Colonel Lathrop would have none of it.

"We'll shelter here or inside the blockhouses," he said. "They can't attack until they stop firing their cannon, and then our rifles can pick them off before they cross the open stretch all around." What Lathrop failed to consider was that since we had cannons on every side, the Rebs could lob shells into the compound without regard to the bulwarks.

A mass of milling figures on horseback surged into view in front of one battery. Presently a white cloth floated aloft, tied to the end of a saber.

"Parley!" Lathrop yelled. "Hold your fire! Let's hear what they have to say."

"Lathrop likely thinks they'll be wantin' to surrender to us," Cate grunted.

Accompanied by an escort of four troopers, a tall man on a black horse cantered toward the gates. He reined up at a distance of some fifty yards and hollered for the commander.

"I command here," Lathrop responded, his tone prideful and haughty. "Colonel William H. Lathrop. And whom do I have the honor of addressing?"

He must have been the only man in the fort who did not already know the answer.

"Gen'rl Nathan Bedford Forrest," was the reply. "Suh, as you see, yore position is surrounded and untenable. I beg you to prevent unnecessary loss of life by surrendering now."

Whether pride, fear for the fate of his black soldiers, or genuine though ill-considered confidence caused Lathrop's decision, I cannot say. His reply was abrupt and offhand: "Never! If you think you can achieve my position, then sir, come and take it!"

Before Forrest and his honor guard had returned to their ranks, the bombardment began. With a precise cadence, like a formal salute at a funeral, eight cannons boomed in turn. The very first shell landed on top of a blockhouse and blew a hole through the roof.

Crouching down in the dirt of the embankment, I used my saber to scratch out a depression in the earth into which I could fold myself. All around me, everyone was doing the same.

After the first volley, there was no rhythm to the guns. The explosions of their charges rolled over and on top of one another, as if each gun crew was competing to see who could fire rounds the fastest. It was like thunder, only without a letup. It was like a barn being struck by lightning, over and over and over.

A solid shot hit the earthwork just on the other side of me. Had the cannonball struck six inches higher, it would have taken my head off. Another round crashed into a blockhouse, punching completely through the wall like an auger. The batteries fired solid shot, exploding shot, canister, and grapeshot, using every shell that came to hand it seemed.

Once when I was very young, I wrestled with my brother for the possession of a fishing pole on the bank of the Tennessee River. Clutching the prize, we both fell into the current. He surfaced at once, and since we could both swim like fish, he made it easily back to shore. But I was swept by the current under a bank. My ankle caught in the forked root of a half-submerged willow. I could not free myself by going either up or down, and to move back against the current was impossible. Finally, just before I gave in and sucked water into my lungs, my struggles broke the root and freed my ankle. I floated downstream to a sandy shore. My brother helped haul me out, and I lay there, more drowned than alive. We never told of that experience, for fear of getting whupped. Afterward I forced myself to overcome the fear and made myself be a strong swimmer in spite of it.

Being under that bombardment was like drowning. There was no way to fight back, and there was no escape. Breathing became labored. I gasped for breath and held each one, as if sucking in a single puff of air would draw a shell. The ground wavered under my feet and tossed me about like waves. The air was foul with the stench of gunpowder and smoke. The crash of the shells was so numbing that everyone was deafened, and I found an opportunity to be grateful for my own lessened hearing. I could still feel every concussion, and it was as though the rounds were bursting inside my head, inside my stomach, and inside my legs.

I saw Colonel Lathrop shouting orders from the entrance to one of the blockhouses. An instant later a shell exploded above the center of the compound, and the colonel paid the price for his foolish arrogance. Shrapnel ripped him to pieces, and his body, though momentarily upright, appeared to have been savaged by wolves.

Another exploding shell bounded into the fort with its fuse still sputtering. It ricocheted off the top of the earthwork and spun to a stop no more than thirty feet from me.

Hamilton and I saw the bomb at the same instant. Before I could move or even think, Hamilton shouted, "Look out, Jesse!" He threw himself over my body, covering it with his own.

The shell detonated then. Hamilton and I were tossed into the air and tumbled in a heap. By the time I collected my dazed wits, it was clear that he was dying. "Glad . . . I'm ready . . . to go," he said. "God bless . . ." And he was gone.

There was no time to grieve. Our commander tried to rally us for an attack. "Mount up!" Colonel Minnis urged. "Mount up, before we are all slaughtered in here!"

The horses were panicked and surged back and forth across the compound with every explosion. I laid my hand on the broken lead rope around the neck of one, only to have it struck by a shell fragment and die at the end of the tether. Minnis then tried to organize an attack on foot. "Captain Briant!" he called. "Have your men form up beside the gate. We'll rush the battery near the blackberry thicket. We must have something with which to fight back! We can turn captured guns on the Rebs!"

There was not a chance we would have ever survived such a rush. Before we crossed half the distance to the Reb position, they would have mowed us down with grape and canister.

As it was, the charge was never even launched. Another exploding shell detonated on the wall of the blockhouse right behind Minnis. The wooden wall absorbed much of the impact, but a chunk of metal rebounded from the blow and hit the colonel in the back of the head. He fell senseless to the ground.

For two hours and, as I heard later, over eight hundred rounds of ammunition, the carnage continued. Then the roar fell silent.

Again General Forrest approached under a flag of truce. "Will you surrender the fort now?" he yelled.

"Colonel Lathrop is dead," Captain Briant replied, "and Colonel Minnis is badly wounded. But I accept your offer."

"Stack yore arms and come out," Forrest ordered, and so we did.

Old Bedford had captured Sulphur Branch Trestle intact. Besides four hundred dead and wounded, and the rest of us taken prisoner, he also collected three hundred horses. Of his own command, nary a single man was hurt or killed.

Forrest allowed us to gather in burial details and give our dead proper treatment. Carrying the bodies out of the fort, I walked near the Reb general several times. I wondered if he would recognize me as the deserter from his forced Nashville recruiting or if he connected me with the death of his brother, Jeffrey. Perhaps my gaunt, smoke-stained face was unrecognizable or perhaps he let it pass. Either way, he said nothing. Perhaps his mind was occupied with the hundreds of repeating rifles he had suddenly acquired: One-fourth of his men had begun the Middle Tennessee campaign without any firearms at all. Old Bedford had promised to see them fitted out, and he had delivered.

When the burying was done and the wounded made ready for travel, we formed up in marching columns to go into captivity. All the Negro soldiers were sent off separately from the rest . . . I do not know what became of them.

CHAPTER 10

CAHABA PRISON
SEPTEMBER 1864–
APRIL 1865

When we were herded away from the burned-out hulk of the fort, I had no idea where we were going. Our captors rode while we walked, and they were anxious for us to hurry. It seems that Forrest had requested Confederate provost guards to accompany his prisoners and been refused.

There was nothing for it but to divide his command and use some of his own troops as wardens. Since Forrest's raid was headed on into Middle Tennessee, he could hardly spare any men. The result was that he was in a foul mood, and the men detailed to accompany us were in no great spirits either. They were in a lather to get us into somebody else's keeping and get back to the foray.

They hiked us overland to Cherokee Station, a distance of sixty weary miles. Covering the distance in forced marches took only three days. We carried our own wounded and had only hardtack bread to eat. Our escorts relieved us of all our other supplies and rations but were prevented by their officers from stealing our clothing, boots, or personal belongings.

On the second day they allowed us to fall out for five minutes of rest beside a slough covered in green scum. While the guards filled their canteens from the only clear spring, we were forced to drink our fill from the swamp.

That night and all the next day, full two-thirds of those captured were deathly ill with the flux. It made no difference to the attitude of the guards. If a man had to fall out of the column because of an urgent sickness it was permitted, but thereafter he was made to stagger at bayonet point to catch up.

I was one of the afflicted. Dazed from the shelling, numbed because of the death of young Hamilton, wearied to the point of collapse by the march, and then sapped of any reserve through the action of the distemper, I was near the end of my string.

Captain Briant found me lying beside the road. I was facedown in a pool of mud not over two inches deep but like to drown there just the same. "Come on, Jesse," he urged. "Get up, man."

"I don't think I can, Cap."

"Sure you can. Dobbs, lend a hand here."

The remaining leagues of our trek are only a blur in my memory. I know that Dobbs and the captain supported me between them. As for the ground we crossed, I cannot recover any particle of my own recollection, except for one snatch of conversation. During another all too brief respite for stale water and weevily bread, Dobbs and the captain leaned me back against a fence post, and I slid downward. The captain went off to demand fresh drinking water for the men while Dobbs knelt beside me.

"Jesse," he said, "you gonna make it?"

I shook my head ponderously. Even that little movement seemed like too much effort. "I'm mighty used up," I said. "Don't know how you keep goin' and carry me at the same time."

"It ain't nothin'," he shrugged. Then, "Say, Jesse, do you still got that letter and watch I give you to keep for me?"

Reaching inside my tunic to search for the packet, I overbalanced sideways and would have sprawled on the ground had not Dobbs caught me. I drew out the parcel with trembling fingers. "Here it is."

"Thanks," he said, then with embarrassment, "Guess I was wrong about it bein' my time."

My eyelids would barely remain open enough for me to focus on his face, but I gave my best effort. "It *was* for lots of others," I said, remembering Hamilton's sacrifice.

"Been thinking about that," he said. "I still don't know why I lived. Why me?"

Slurring my words could not be prevented, but I answered anyway. "Maybe because God was gracious and knew you weren't ready to face Him . . . and maybe because He still has important things for you to do here."

Dobbs nodded slowly. "'Spose it could be both?"

Nodding was the best response I could manage, but he seemed satisfied. Soon Captain Briant returned. We were rationed one canteen of fresh water among every three men, but it was better than before.

Another fifty men died on the march.

At the rail yard at Cherokee Station we were crowded into a stockade like so many head of cattle, along with other prisoners gathered by Forrest's sweep through northern Alabama. Guards patrolled a narrow catwalk atop the board fence. On our part, we milled around ceaselessly because there were so many prisoners crammed into the space there was no room to sit or lie down.

On our third day in the corral we met a provost guard named Mills. He was an unshaven, snaggle-toothed rascal with a head shaped like a cannonball and an intellect to match. His eye gleamed with a native shrewdness and gave him a crafty, furtive look.

"Psst," he hissed at Dobbs from the platform. "You got big feet, same as me. Give you a loaf of bread for them shoes o'yourn." He wiggled his toes to show where his own footgear had worn through.

"My boots?" Dobbs argued. "What'm I gonna march in then?"

"Y'all are goin' by train," Mills corrected. "Can you eat them shoes, or do you want the bread?"

Dobbs passed up the boots and got a lumpy, dark brown loaf of bread in return. It was coarse and the texture full of grit, but it was better than anything we had eaten for six days.

The exchange gave Captain Briant an idea.

The next night only Mills and one other guard were on watch. When the two sentries were the farthest apart, Briant hailed Mills. "Private," he called. "How'd you like to get a solid gold watch?"

Mills's eyes lit up with greed. "Whatcha want fer it?" he asked without hesitation.

"There's over a thousand of us in here," Briant said. "You know we haven't been registered yet, and nobody will know if a few go missing. If you look the other way while ten of us slip out the gate, the watch is yours."

"Not no officers," Mills protested. "They'll have my guts for garters if'n I lose an officer."

"All right," Briant said without hesitation. "Ten of my men, then."

"Three," was the sharp reply.

"Six," responded Briant. "And now, tonight, or the deal is off." Briant pointed out five other men and me. "You six will break out tonight. Due north will take you to the river. Follow it east and you'll find one of our patrols in a day or so."

I was already shaking my head. "God bless you, Captain, but I can't go," I said. "Send someone else in my place. I'd never make it as far as the river."

Captain Briant looked me in the eyes for a long moment, then nodded and named another to go in my place. Six shadows flitted out beyond the faint light of the torches and disappeared in the darkness. Then Briant whispered, "Anybody else have a watch or valuable to barter? More of you can make the attempt."

Dobbs extracted his pocket watch and chain and passed it to the captain. "Use mine," he said.

The negotiation with Mills was even briefer. The captain said to Dobbs, "It's your watch, Private. You name the others to accompany you."

"You pick 'em, Captain," Dobbs replied. "And go on and name six. If Jesse can't leave, reckon I'll stay with him."

Six more of our men slipped away in the night.

The next morning it was announced that officers were to be sent to a different prison from the enlisted men and that all of us were shipping out that very day. "Good-bye, Corporal," Briant said to me. "I'll pray for you."

"And I for you, Captain," I said.

When they loaded us aboard cattle cars, a hundred to a car, the remaining members of Company F were all crammed in together: me, Dobbs, Sergeant Cate, and fifteen more from other messes. Out of a hundred men plus replacements, all the rest were gone.

—————◆—————

Before the rebellion, Cahaba Prison had not been a prison. It had not been a jail, a stockade, or a barracks . . . it had been a cotton warehouse. Located on the west bank of the Alabama River, Cahaba was a dilapidated high-roofed shed and a muddy slope open to the rain. Where there had once been docks and loading platforms, these had been torn down and a fence taller than a man could reach reared from waist-deep, brown water. There were guards on the roof and on a walkway that surrounded the compound. We were only ten miles south of Selma, Alabama, but we might as well have been in darkest Africa, so far from anything like civilization did we feel.

When we arrived I could hardly walk, but after the cramped transport in the cattle cars, neither could anyone else. Dobbs and I leaned toward each other like a pair of drunks. It took two hours for our captors to move us from the rail siding into the prison.

Once inside, a pair of iron-barred gates slammed shut behind us. A Reb officer yelled, "Line up fer rations! Move along lively now!"

We all shuffled forward as best we were able, approaching a long, narrow table heaped with cornmeal and dried peas. As each prisoner neared the counter, a double handful of each foodstuff was poured into his haversack, if he still had one, or into his cupped hands or shirttails if he did not. A chunk of green salt beef furnished the rest of our allowance.

Sergeant Cate squinted a bloodshot eye at the dirty, yellow meal spilling from his grimy hands and asked, "Would this be dinner or supper you're issuing here?"

The greasy-faced corporal ladling out the grain laughed. "What are you thinkin', Billy Yank? That there is all you gonna get till tomorrow this time . . . if you're lucky."

"And what are we supposed to be cooking it in?" Cate continued.

"Well now, that'd be yore problem, wouldn't it?"

Cate asked me, "Jesse, would you be having a pan to cook this in?"

I did not, nor was one easily located. When we finally did come across a soldier still carrying a skillet, there was yet another problem to be faced. "Where's the firewood?" Dobbs asked a guard.

"Ask yore Gen'rl Sherman," replied the stoney-faced sentry. "He's been burnin' houses and such clean across Georgia, so we don't let you Yanks play with no fire."

We were permitted to build campfires on the clay slope that ran down to the river, if firewood could be located. For a price—Yankee dollars, gold watches or jewelry—our wardens would part with a few miserable pieces of wood that burned with very little heat.

The first night we followed the practice of most of the prisoners: We stirred the meal into a tin cup of water and drank it. When weevils floated up out of the meal Cate's response was, "Don't be complainin' about that. It's better than the other meat in this rathole."

There was something like two thousand prisoners in Cahaba, despite the fact that it had only been planned to house three hundred. Worse yet, for most of the war Cahaba had only been a transfer point for Yankees being shipped elsewhere. After the loss of Atlanta and the slicing in two of the Confederacy, Cahaba was now bursting its seams.

Cate, Dobbs, and I, as some of the later arrivals, could find no place under the roofed shed. We pitched our camp on an unoccupied stretch of clay hillside; that's all the decision there was to be made.

———>◆<———

By the winter of 1865, it was clear to everyone in Cahaba, prisoners and guards both, that the war was not going well for the Confederacy. Just before Christmas in '64, Sherman completed his march to the sea by swallowing up Savannah. His army destroyed hundreds of miles of railroad track, turning the rails into "Sherman hairpins" by bending heated steel around tree stumps. Hundreds of liberated slaves followed in his wake, even as Sherman turned north trailing a swath of destruction toward Columbia, South Carolina.

Up north, Grant had Lee pinned behind his defenses at Petersburg. While Grant's men kept warm and snug in their solid bombproofs, the Rebs starved, suffered from the icy blasts, and deserted in droves.

Despite the captured Spencer rifles, Nathan Bedford Forrest was driven back. The high tide of the Confederate Army of Tennessee crested at Nashville, there to be thrown into confusion. They retreated, a disordered rabble.

The worse the news from the Rebel front, the

harsher our treatment became. No longer were we given any opportunity to wash our clothes except in the filthy, muddy river. We pleaded to be allowed one pair of scissors so that we could crop our hair, but this was denied us. Lice multiplied and spread throughout the camp. Our jailers no longer entered the compound with our supplies; they merely tossed the sacks over the wall to be pounced on by us like so many animals.

Our daily ration of dried peas was stopped, then our quarter pound of salt meat was limited to every other day, and then it was halted altogether. We lived on a quart of cornmeal a day, baked if we had a pan, boiled in tin cans, or stirred up in cold water and drank if no other means presented itself.

The short rations made us lose weight until our bones almost protruded through the skin. Cate, Dobbs, and I managed to keep warm enough and sheltered inside our poor tent. I had remained miraculously free of illness, despite the harsh treatment. I reminded myself of my promise to Alcie: I must get home to her again, I had given my word on it.

Then came the rains.

For the first two weeks of March it rained almost continuously. Sergeant Cate and Dobbs were careful of my health and demanded that I keep close and not expose myself unnecessarily to the damp and the harsh winds.

The river rose.

It encroached on two feet of the mud bank the first

day, driving back those encamped on the verge. We were all squeezed into a smaller space. The next day the climbing Alabama River reclaimed ten feet of its shoreline from the Yankee invaders, and we retreated still more; cold water, no dry place, no firewood.

For three more days the river continued to rise. Passing the highest flood crest ever remembered in those parts, the swell lapped inside the old warehouse building itself.

Those nearest the iron grate hammered and screamed to be let out. They were smashed against the locked portal by those displaced by the water. Six men were crushed to death by the press of the mob. The rest of us stood in water up to our knees, with no escape.

That was when our guards disappeared.

Perhaps they were fearful for their lives. Perhaps they thought that such a mass of men as we would overpower the bars and force an escape.

Perhaps they had no authority to move us and preferred not to see what was happening.

Whatever the reason, all our wardens went away. If we had possessed the strength, we could have freed the entire prison, but of course we had not the means. Along with the guards went any hope of medical treatment and the last of the paltry rations.

Some prisoners went mad and drowned themselves. Some just died standing up, starved to death or sick. No one came to remove the bodies.

After a time, hunger retreated to become a gnawing

ache and a hollow place inside. But to stand in two feet of muck with nothing to drink is torture beyond belief.

After three days with no food and no clean water, I drank from the river.

That night my head pounded like it was the anvil underneath the hammers of all the blacksmiths in the world. My neck stiffened until I could not turn my head. Lights began flashing in front of my eyes, and I could no longer make out the features of my friends.

I knew that Cate and Dobbs took turns about holding me on their shoulders so as to raise me for a time above the flood. It was only because I had shrunk to ninety-five pounds that they could do so at all. My legs were so swollen and my frame so shrunken that I resembled a man stuck together of mismatched halves.

Sleep was all I had left, but even it was a torment. William appeared before my eyes, only to be shot, or drowned, or stabbed before I could reach him. I saw my home in flames, Alcie and the little ones turned out on the road in the rain. My fever raged, and delirium played on me like the cascade of a waterfall striking rocks below, splintering me into a thousand unconnected fragments.

I thought I heard someone say, "Oh, God, don't let him die. Not now! Not now!"

Am I dying? I wondered. *It is news to me that I am still alive now. Is this only another dream?*

"Now that I've found him, don't let him die!" the voice implored the Almighty.

Summoning up my last reserve of strength, I opened one eye and croaked, "Not dead just yet."

Staring down at me was a thin, bearded stranger; a young man by the sparse, fine whiskers. He seemed to be someone I knew, but could not place . . . someone from a long time before.

"Father!" he said. "Don't you know me? It's William."

⋖＞◈＜⋗

There is still a little more to tell.

William had been shifted from one Confederate prison to another, always being moved south. He was never allowed to be exchanged because a Tellico Junction neighbor, fighting for the Rebs, had denounced him for helping runaway slaves. Cahaba was the sixth confinement he had suffered since his capture.

Before William came to Cahaba, the water had receded, and I had been removed from the prison to a hospital bed. A new commander had been appointed by the Rebs, and he, knowing the end of the Confederacy was near, was fearful of Union reprisals if conditions were not improved.

I had been in a stupor for weeks, but after my son's arrival I knew I would live.

Lee surrendered in Virginia, and then Joe Johnston did the same with the remnant of the Reb Army of Tennessee. We heard that Forrest thought about fleeing to Mexico and continuing the fight, but in the end he, too, surrendered.

The war was over.

As soon as I was able, I sent a joyful message to Athens, to be delivered care of R. J. Ferguson, Tellico Junction, to Mrs. Jesse Dodson: "Found William. Am coming home. Kept both promises."

I was still too weak to even stand, let alone walk, so I was transported by river to the army hospital in Vicksburg, Mississippi, where I was formally released from captivity.

William never left my side. The progress of my illness was not steady, with many ups and downs. For a while I thought I was completely deaf before I regained some hearing in my right ear. I also was fearful that I would never walk again, but in time the dropsy subsided, and the paralysis also passed.

William and I were slated to go north to Camp Chase in Ohio to be mustered out. We had our passage arranged on a steamer and were excited about being that much nearer home. Then I took a turn for the worse, and we could not go.

Urging William, I said, "I'm on the mend now. Get home to your mother. Tell her I'll be along soon as I'm able."

Despite my insistence, he refused. He always was a headstrong boy.

That night, the *Sultana,* the steamer which was to have taken us north, blew up on the river. Her boiler exploded, and fifteen hundred men, all returning Yankee prisoners of war, were scalded to death or drowned.

The Almighty had plenty of opportunities to take my life, but instead He used Hamilton, Dobbs, Sergeant Cate, and finally my boy William to keep giving it back to me.

A very different man crossed back over the Cumberland Mountains in the summer of 1865 than had journeyed there two years before. I resolved never to forget what I had learned, what I had been given.

HISTORICAL NOTE

Despite being wounded nine times and having forty horses shot out from under him, Nathan Bedford Forrest survived the war. One of the most enigmatic figures of the American Civil War, he can truly be described as alternately chivalrous, cruel, coarse, daring, hot-tempered, brilliant, and harsh. An unremarkable postwar businessman, Forrest went on to achieve notoriety in another way. Though it was never publicly acknowledged, Old Bedford was reputedly the first Grand Wizard of the Ku Klux Klan.

Jesse Dodson and his son returned home to Tellico Junction. Though completely deaf in one ear and partially so in the other, and regardless of lifelong bouts with rheumatism, dysentery, and heart disease, Jesse lived to be ninety-three. In all he and Alcie had nine children. Three of these were born after the war, one of them being Brock's great-grandmother.

ABOUT THE AUTHORS

With twenty-four novels to their credit, more than six million books in print, and eight ECPA Gold Medallion awards, Bodie and Brock Thoene have taken their works of historical fiction to the top of the best-seller charts and to the hearts of their readers.

Bodie is the storyteller, weaving plotlines and characters into stunning recreations of bygone eras.

Brock provides the foundation for Bodie's tales. His meticulous research and attention to historical detail ensure that the books are both informative and entertaining.

The Thoenes' collaboration receives critical acclaim as well as high praise from their appreciative audience.

LOOK FOR THESE OTHER BESTSELLING
NOVELS FROM BODIE AND BROCK THOENE

WINDS OF PROMISE

The first book in the Wayward Wind Series deposits the reader onto the life of Rafer Maddox and the gold rush fever that gripped San Francisco on the 1850s. Maddox stumbles onto a deadly ring of thievery that threatens all he loves, and brings his soul closer to the will of the Almighty.

0-7852-8072-3 • 224 pages • Trade Paperback

TO GATHER THE WIND

Twenty-six-year-old Jack Ryland suddenly finds himself in the middle of a manhunt and murder investigation. The search for clues takes Jack to the untamed country of Coloma, the birthplace of the California Gold Rush. The second book in the Wayward Wind Series takes readers out to the old West with heart-stopping action and colorful characters.

0-7852-8073-1 • 224 pages • Trade Paperback

SHILOH AUTUMN

The most heartfelt book the Thoenes have written, this novel is a compelling portrait of an American dust bowl family. Based on Bodie's own grandparents' lives, *Shiloh Autumn* takes readers back to the Great Depression to experience Depression-era life, from possum hunts to mass migration, Penny Auctions to the Veterans' March on Washington. Another Thoene novel destined to become a classic.

0-7852-8066-9 • 480 pages • Hardcover
0-7852-7134-1 • 480 pages • Trade Paperback
0-7852-7273-9 • Audio